KE... WHAT'S HIS

KEEPING WHAT'S HIS

PORTER BROTHERS TRILOGY: TATE

Book One

JAMIE BEGLEY

Young Ink Press Publication
YoungInkPress.com

Copyright © 2015 by Jamie Begley

ISBN-10: 0692615490
ISBN-13: 9780692615492

Edited by C&D Editing, Hot Tree Editing, and Bippity Boppity
Book
Cover Art by Young Ink Press

This book is a work of fiction. Names, characters, places, and
incidents either are products of the author's imagination or are
used fictitiously. Any resemblance to actual persons, living or dead,
events, or locales is entirely coincidental.

*This work of fiction is intended for mature audiences only. All sexually
active characters portrayed in this ebook are eighteen years of age or older.
Please do not buy if strong sexual situations, violence, drugs, domestic abuse,
child abuse, and explicit language offends you.*

Connect with Jamie,
JamieBegley@ymail.com
www.facebook.com/AuthorJamieBegley
www.JamieBegley.net

PROLOGUE

Tate yawned as he went into the kitchen to turn out the light before going to bed. His hand was on the switch when a sound he hadn't heard since he was eighteen reached his ears. A chill stiffened his spine at the distinctive melody only a few members in his family tree had been gifted to hear.

Changing directions, he went to the front door, taking the shotgun off the rack, opening the door to stride out onto the lit front porch. It was still muggy and the summer night was eerily silent. Tate's eyes surveyed his land, looking for anything out of place. He pumped his rifle, waiting to shoot anything stupid enough to move. Tresspassers would recognize the distinctive sound.

"What's wrong?" Greer's low voice alerted him to his presence as he moved to stand next to him, rifle held expertly in his hands.

"Don't know," Tate answered, not taking his eyes off the trees bordering their house.

Greer didn't question his instincts. In their profession, their lives and those of the ones in the house depended on their staying alert to possible danger.

Dustin's shadow was the next to join his brothers, his rifle pointed at the dark woods.

"Want me to go check the field?" Dustin asked.

"No," Tate answered sharply. "I will. Greer, you keep an eye outside. Dustin, you go back inside with Holly and Logan." He took a step off the porch, pausing with his back to his brothers. "I heard the death bell."

"Shit! How many times?" Dustin's sharp question held worry for his son sleeping in the house.

"Once."

Each of the Porters were gifted, or cursed, depending on which one you talked to. Rachel was the most powerful of the four, having inherited most of their grandmother's gifts. Tate's own power wasn't a gift, but the curse of knowing someone was going to die. He never knew whom Death was going to strike. It could be a family member or someone he had been near recently. The first toll was a warning that Death was coming, the second meant Death had found his victim, and the third was Death's arrival. He had heard the bells intermittently during childhood. He had asked his grandmother about the sounds that no one else seemed able to hear, and she had looked at him sadly, explaining how the death knells were a warning.

"How do I know who's gonna die?" he had asked.

"You don't."

"Then what good is it?"

"It's a warning to keep your family safe. Don't let Death sneak in the backdoor to steal what's yours."

Tate had taken his grandmother's words to heart. Whenever he heard the bells, he became vigilant, watching over his family until Death's next victim was revealed. However, only once had he known whom the bells were intended for, and that was his grandmother. She had been ill for some time. He had gone to her late one night when he had heard the second bell, giving her the warning she had known was coming.

"I'm ready." Her weary voice had been filled with pain as she had taken his hand and held it while he sat by her bedside. "Tate, one day, you're going to be head of this family. It's your job to make sure everyone's kept safe. Don't let me down."

"I won't, Grandma," Tate had promised.

He had failed in that promise with his mother and father, neither listened to his warning to stay home the day they had gone fishing. It had taken a week of dragging the river to find their bodies. Since then, he hadn't heard the death knells.

He took the last step off the porch, striding across the yard to head into the dark woods. He knew the mountain like the back of his hand, so he easily maneuvered through the thick brush for over a mile, avoiding the traps set to catch trespassers who wanted to steal what they had spent all season growing, which was worth a small fortune. He listened to every noise, trying to pinpoint whether anything was moving, but could hear nothing.

Crouching, he scooted under a heavy patch of briars until he came out on the other side, looking around the massive field of marijuana he and his brothers had planted. Next week, they would cut it then dry it out in their homemade drying shed. It was their winter supply. They wouldn't start growing again until next spring.

Tate wished now he hadn't listened to Dustin to give it an extra week to grow. They should have cut and processed it last week, but Dustin wanted Logan out of the house while they processed the pot in the barn. In three days Logan would be leaving to stay with his great-grandmother in town. They could get the weed dried out and bagged before he returned from the two-week stay.

Tate didn't see anything out of place. None of the traps had been touched. He walked around the perimeter of the field, unable to explain the uneasy feeling. If it was daylight, he would climb a tree and look out over the area, but the darkness made that option useless.

Quietly, he went back through the opening in the briars, coming out the other end where he carefully removed any signs that he had passed through. Standing, he made his way back to the house.

"Find anything?" Greer asked when he was back on the porch.

"Nothing. You see or hear anything?"

"Nope. Think the bells just got you spooked?"

"No, someone's out there."

"Want me to take watch?" Greer's own eyes searched the woods surrounding the house.

"No. Go inside. I'll keep watch until morning. At daylight, I want Holly and Logan out of here. Take them to Mrs. Langley's a few days early."

"I'll tell Dustin." Greer turned to go inside. "He won't be happy. He misses him when he's gone."

"I'm not taking chances. The Hayeses and Colemans are still pissed off no one's buying the shit they're growing, and they're taking more chances selling it to out-of-town buyers."

"I saw Asher and Holt in town the other day talking to Shade."

Tate stiffened. "Do you think The Last Riders are buying from them?"

The bikers were his best buyers, but between them and selling to the people in the county and across the state line, they sometimes ran short.

"I'll talk to him and find out."

"If the Hayeses have been selling to Shade when we run short, they could be thinking about taking us out to get the whole fucking pie."

"That's what I'm thinking. I'm not worried about the Colemans; they couldn't stick a finger up their own ass, much less take us out." Greer's scorn for the Colemans was deep rooted. Tate often found himself breaking up the fights Greer had started with them.

"Asher and Holt, on the other hand, can do some damage. Asher is a mean asshole, and Holt's a sneaky son of a bitch," Tate reminded him.

"I'll get in touch with Shade first thing in the morning."

"Do that. I'm going to call Cash and tell him to watch Rachel."

"You think someone would be stupid enough to make a move on Rachel to get at us?"

"I'm not taking any chances," Tate said grimly.

Greer nodded. "Night. I'll see you in the morning."

"Night."

When Greer went inside, Tate sat down on the porch. He couldn't relax while waiting to see if one of their enemies would strike. It was times like this he wished he had listened to his mother and Rachel. The other dealers in their area were envious of their crop and connections, and would do anything to bring them down, even if it meant taking out his entire family. He would probably have stopped dealing already, but Greer wasn't ready to give it up. They had accumulated too many enemies over the years, and his brother believed if they stopped providing product, their customers would go with another dealer who would push them toward harder drugs to fatten the dealers' wallets.

They had managed to keep blue heroin out of Treepoint, but it was becoming a deadly struggle that he wasn't sure they were going to win. He heard a rumor the Colemens were dealing Spice, a synthetic marijuana that fucked up those who used it. The effects lasted longer and were much stronger than marijuana, which had the buyers wanting to buy more from their dealer. Many of those buyers were in high school and often ended up in the emergency room. He and his brother had two rules when selling: don't sell to kids, and make damn sure they weren't a Fed. The constant demand for their product put them in jeopardary from the other dealers in the county. As head of the family, it was his job to protect them. So far, he had succeeded, but constant worries were leaving him uneasy.

His premonitions were never wrong. Like a massive storm brewing, no one could know the devastating effect until it struck. Tate's hand tightened on his shotgun. He had been born and bred on this mountain, and no one was taking what was his without a fight.

Chapter One

"When do you leave?"

Sutton looked up from the document in her hand, placing it back down on the desk before answering her friend. "As soon as I clear the rest of my paperwork," she said wryly, looking at the large stack of papers still waiting for her signature.

"I still can't understand why you're going to Treepoint, Kentucky for your vacation. You could go anywhere."

"I have been everywhere. Besides, I miss Treepoint, and I need to figure out what I'm going to do with my grandfather's house." She would use the time she was staying there to decide whether she wanted to fix up the run-down property or sell it, breaking the last connection to her hometown.

"Why would you want to keep it? Your life is here in California."

What life? Sutton thought to herself.

"I can do my job anywhere there's internet." Sutton shrugged off her roommate's concern. "What, Treepoint doesn't appeal to you? You could go with me. You have plenty of hours saved up." She tried not to smile when Stella's expression turned to one of horror.

"Over my dead body! What's the population there, three?"

This time, Sutton didn't hold back her smile. "A little more than that, but it doesn't have a mall or the nightclubs you love."

"Then that's a definite no." Stella smoothed back her already perfectly styled hair with her manicured hand. "Are you going to see your dad while you're there?"

"No, and I've told you not to call him my dad." Sutton's voice was ice-cold.

Stella winced. "Sorry." She waved her hand airily. "It's getting embarrassing turning all his calls away."

"Then tell him to quit calling." Sutton began signing the paperwork she had already read through and making notes on those orders that needed to be recounted. Then she handed the pile to Stella when she was finished. "That's it. You sure you don't mind dropping those off at the office for me on your way to work tomorrow?"

"It's only a few blocks away, and I can see that hot boss of yours. It will make my whole fucking day."

"Just don't be late to work. You're already on probation," she warned.

Stella winced. "Don't remind me. You just had to take the fun out of it, didn't you?"

"That's what I'm here for." She rose from her desk and stretched. She had begun working early so she would have plenty of time to get on the road and get at least six hours of driving in before dark. Even after all these years of being away from Kentucky, her body still clung to the time zone that was three hours ahead, sending her to bed long before others in the evening and rising early in the morning, which worked well with her work schedule that dealt with various time zones.

"I'll keep in touch on my drive in."

"You better. I don't want to have to come up there and check on you." She shuddered in mock horror. "You should have some fun, maybe fuck someone. It could improve your sense of humor."

"I'll be too busy cleaning up the house to have any fun, at least for a couple of weeks."

Sutton hugged her good-bye before picking up her purse. "Make sure the house is locked up when you leave. I'm going to be worried about you while I'm gone. Who's going to remind you not to be late or set the alarm?"

"Hopefully your boss," she wisecracked.

"Just don't get me fired for forgetting about that paperwork," she reminded her again.

"I won't. Be careful, Sutton."

"Always." Sutton headed outside of her large home to the car she had rented. Her own car sat in the garage, it would stick out like a sore thumb in Treepoint, and didn't want to draw attention while in her hometown. The only person she intended to see had no idea she was coming, and certainly wouldn't welcome her back. She was determined to see Rachel Porter and set things straight. Only then could she finally leave the weight of the past behind to move forward with her life.

Sutton put the key in the ignition, her stomach already clenching with nerves. Sliding her sunglasses on, she put the car in drive.

Her hometown had been calling her more and more each day. The constant niggling feeling becoming more forcefull, wearing on her determination to stay away. It was time to answer the call.

CHAPTER TWO

"Who's that?" Tate turned at Greer's low whistle.

He glanced in the direction that Greer nodded his head, seeing a woman pull a red suitcase from the trunk of her car before slamming the trunk closed. Both men watched as the slim brunette rolled the suitcase to the hotel door, sliding the card into the card reader.

"I don't know," Tate answered his brother. There was something vaguely familiar about the way the woman moved, but Tate couldn't place her, and was unable to get a clear view of her face.

"Do you think she's staying long?"

"How in the fuck would I know? Let's get these groceries loaded. We need to get home. I don't like leaving Dustin home alone for long."

The brothers finished loading the groceries into the bed of their truck before climbing into the cab. His eyes went to the closed hotel door the woman had entered. He had no idea who she was, but Tate could understand his brother's interest. The woman had on a pair of shorts and a T-shirt that had showed her tanned skin and perky ass. If her face was half as good, Greer would be in Heaven. The man got a hard-on for brunettes, while Tate preferred fair-haired women. He had only dated one brunette, and she was a memory he wished he could forget.

Tate drove the old pick-up toward the mountains where their house was located.

"You going out tonight?"

"No, why?"

"Thought I would meet Diane at Rosie's," Greer explained.

"Why do you want to step in that dog shit? We have enough enemies without you adding her to the mix."

"She swears she isn't seeing anyone except me," Greer argued.

"Which doesn't mean shit and you know it. That lying whore would swear on a stack of bibles she was a virgin if she had a reason. You want to piss the Hayeses off? I heard she's been fucking around with Asher."

"There isn't going to be a fight. He didn't start a fight when she was hanging around The Last Riders, so why would he give me trouble?"

"Maybe because you don't have a clubhouse of bikers backing you up," Tate replied.

"I don't need those pussies to back me up. I have my rifle, you, and Dustin." Greer looked at him from the corner of his eye. "Besides, she told me she hasn't seen him in a couple of months."

Tate's mouth tightened into a grim line, knowing Greer would do what he wanted, regardless of the consequences. Greer would never back down from trouble, and sometimes, he deliberately sought it out. This was one of those times.

He sighed. "Try not to shove it in their faces."

"Why would I do that?" Greer gave him a shit-eating grin.

"Because it's what you do. This time, I'm telling you to take it easy. If you get us all killed, do you want Holly raising Logan alone?"

Greer lost his grin. "That will never happen. I'll see to that."

"Not if your ass is buried six feet under," Tate said as he carefully maneuvered the truck up the rutted driveway that led to their house.

"Isn't going to happen. I don't know why we still need her hanging around, anyway."

"Because Logan's attached to her. To him, she's his mother."

Tate didn't harbor any ill-will toward Holly. He had saved all his hate for Samantha Langley, Logan's biological mother who hadn't told Dustin he had knocked her up in high school. Her father had taken her to Jamestown where she had the child in secret. Then he had hired Holly to care for the child, leaving her alone to raise Logan, while Samantha returned to Treepoint without anyone in town realizing she had a child. When Samantha died, Holly hadn't told anyone of Logan's existence to afraid of losing the child that had become like her own. If not for Diamond, the town lawyer, defending her now husband Knox, Tate doubted they would have ever found him. Holly planned to leave town when she discovered what inherited illness was making Logan so sick. Greer wouldn't forgive her for her deceit in keeping Logan hidden.

"He's old enough that we don't need her anymore."

"You going to drag your ass out of bed to take him to school in the mornings? Wash his dirty clothes? Fix his dinner? I don't notice you putting up a fight when Holly washes your dirty clothes, and you sure as fuck don't have a problem wolfing down those meals she cooks."

Greer shrugged. "She's earning her keep."

Tate snorted. "What keep? That small bedroom she sleeps in, or the house where you refuse to remodel the kitchen? The floorboards are so thin one of us will go through them one day."

"It's fine." Greer crossed his arms against his chest stubbornly.

"It's a shithole, and you know it, but you're hoping to run Holly off. I thought you were smarter than that. Holly won't leave Logan. She'd die for that boy, which is more than I can say about you."

"What in the fuck does that mean?"

"It means, after we sell the pot, we're getting a new kitchen," Tate stated firmly.

"You'll be using your share, then. I have better uses for my money."

"What? Drinking or whoring?"

"Both."

Tate's hands tightened on the steering wheel, controlling the impulse to punch his brother in the face. Bringing the truck to a stop in front of their house, he turned to stare coldly at Greer.

"We're getting the fucking kitchen."

Greer opened his mouth then closed it, smart enough to realize Tate's mind was made up.

"Fine, but there better not be any fancy shit in it."

Confused, Tate stared at his brother. "Like what?"

"No dishwasher or any of that frosted glass. If I want anyone to see what's in my cabinets, I'll leave the doors open."

Tate laid his head on the steering wheel instead of banging it against it the way he wanted to. "Do you have to be such a hillbilly?"

Greer got out of the truck without answering the obvious.

Tate climbed out after taking a deep breath. Greer would try the patience of a saint, and he sure as fuck wasn't one of those. He lowered the tailgate, pulling the box that held the groceries toward him, and then each brother lifted several bags into their arms.

"You think she'll stay around a while?"

"Holly?"

"No! The woman we saw at the hotel."

His brother had the attention span of a gnat.

"No. She was probably stopping for the night before heading somewhere else."

"I hope not. I'd like to get to know the woman with those tits and ass."

"I don't, and the feeling will be mutual" Tate said, looking over at his brother who was dressed in the faded jeans and work boots he preferred.

Everyone in town thought they were hillbilly trash and wanted nothing to do with them unless they were buying their weekly bag of weed, and the woman he had caught a brief glance of had shouted class and money.

"You never know, I could be her type."

"Not if she has a brain in her head," Tate retorted good-naturedly then laughed when Greer shoved him away from the steps leading up to the front porch. Tate held back, letting Greer go first into the house.

Inside, Dustin got up from the kitchen table where he was working on his computer to help put the groceries away.

"Why did you buy so many groceries?" Dustin asked, opening a bag of chips.

"I don't want to go into town for a while until we find out who's sneaking around at night. If they know we go into town once a week for food, it'll throw them off if we don't go for a while."

"You still think someone's watching the house?" Dustin asked, taking one of the beers before Greer could slide the twelve-pack into the fridge.

"I know so. I just can't figure out who." Tate answered, taking one of the beers for himself.

"Let me get the fucking things cold before you drink them all," Greer complained.

"Have to enjoy them while we can. Holly and Logan will be back soon."

"I don't know why we can't drink beer as long as we don't drink it in front of Logan."

"We all agreed Holly was right, we don't want to give Logan a bad example to follow," Dustin stated as he opened his beer.

"If you're not careful, she'll raise him to be a pussy," Greer griped.

"Shut up. She's right. Ma never let Pa drink in front of us, either."

"And how well did that turn out? Remember that weekend they came home from church and caught us all shit-faced?"

Tate and Dustin both winced at the memory of the ass-whipping their father had given them. He had told all three of them they weren't getting the whipping for getting drunk, but because they were caught by their mother, and he had to listen to her complaints about his beer in the refrigerator.

"Next time, buy your own damn beer," their father had growled before leaving all three of them wailing while he returned to face a furious wife.

"It was worse than the whipping he gave us when he caught us smoking the weed," Dustin remembered.

"Because we were smoking profit. We never did it after that, because he wouldn't give us money for a month." Tate laughed. "Not even lunch money."

"He was a hard-ass," Greer agreed.

"He never had to teach us the same lesson twice," Tate said, lifting the beer to his lips as he looked out the window and saw it was getting dark.

Placing the beer down on the counter, he picked up his shotgun resting near the door. When Logan was home, all the guns were kept in the gun safe except for the one in Tate's holster,

"I'm going to go check the field before it gets dark. I'll be back in an hour. Fry some burgers, Greer."

"Why not Dustin?"

"Because I don't want it burnt," Tate answered, going out the door.

He carefully walked toward the spot where the mairjuana was planted, scanning for any sign of any trespassers. Finding no poachers or issues at the field, he was on his way back to the house when he heard the sound of a motor in the distance. Frowning, he tried to pinpoint the direction of the sound. Quickly he turned on his heels to walk in the opposite direction, maneuvering stealthily through the trees for a quarter of a mile until he came to a stop behind a large tree.

It was almost dark as the car stopped in front of the small house that had stood empty for the last five years. Pap Creech had died, and it had remained untouched since the day the ambulance had taken him away after his heart attack.

The woman from town stood on the porch with a flashlight in her hand. She had changed into jeans and a T-shirt and had pulled her hair back into a tight ponytail.

Tate was about to yell out and tell her she was trespassing when she reached into the pocket of her jeans, pulling out a key and inserting it into the lock.

Tate sucked in a startled breath as she lifted the flashlight higher so she could see the lock, the light illuminating her profile.

Sutton Creech had come home.

CHAPTER THREE

Sutton turned the doorknob. The door didn't want to open, so she braced her shoulder against the door and gave it a hard shove. It still didn't budge.

"Need some help?"

Sutton stiffened at the question coming from the wooded forest. Even after all these years, she recognized the quiet voice without having to turn to see his face.

"I could use the help." Sutton took a step back, turning to the woods to see Tate stepping out from behind a large tree.

His face was shrouded in darkness as Sutton watched him approach the porch indifferently. She had worried about how she would react when she saw him, but she hadn't needed to. The heart he had once sent pounding in her chest didn't skip a beat as he walked past her toward the door.

She caught the scent of the pine trees on him, which was different than the cloying smell of expensive colognes she had become used to.

Sutton watched as Tate pushed the door open then stepped out of the doorway so she could enter without brushing against him. Her mouth quirked at the unnecessary movement. She wasn't anxious to touch him any more than he was to touch her.

"Thanks," she said.

"No problem." He shrugged indifferently. "The electric on?"

"Yes. I called and had the electric company turn it back on last week." Sutton went through the doorway, her hand going familiarly to the wall switch beside the door. Flipping the switch on, she stared around the home that was the same as when she had last been there years before. Everything was covered in dust, and the smell was musty from lack of fresh air, but she didn't notice, too lost in thought.

Tate came to stand next to her, breaking her train of thought.

"How long you staying?"

"I haven't made up my mind yet," Sutton answered.

"Your parents must be glad you've come home for a visit."

Sutton remained quiet as she turned back to the door, placing her hand on the doorknob. "Thanks again for helping me inside."

Tate's brow rose at her abrupt dismissal. Going back through the door, he placed a hand on it before she could close it behind him.

"I wouldn't stay out here too late. It's not safe," he warned.

This time, it was her turn to lift a brow in his direction. "Don't tell me you're still growing weed and keeping poachers away."

Tate's face flushed angrily. "When did you become a bitch?"

Sutton gave him a mocking smile. "I'm not eighteen anymore."

His eyes roved over her body insultingly. "No, you're not. I hope you're not planning on seeing Cash while you're in town. He's married to Rachel now, and I don't want you causing trouble for my sister."

"I know, and I have no intention of seeking out Cash." Sutton lost her smile. Cash wasn't why she was here.

"Good. They're happy, and they don't need you trying to stir up trouble."

"Since you want to talk straight, I'll reciprocate. I'll repeat what I said: I have no intention of seeing Cash. I won't say it was good seeing you again, Tate, because it wasn't." Sutton slammed the door and locked it. She held her breath, listening for sounds from the other side of the door. It was several minutes before she heard him walking away.

Releasing her breath, she turned away from the door and walked farther into the house. It seemed as if her grandfather should have been there, waiting for her; but she heard only silence.

She went to his favorite chair, sitting down and ignoring the dust as she leaned back against the soft leather.

"Pap..." Her voice trailed off, unable to go on with the tears clogging her throat. Her hands tightly gripped the arms of the chair as she gathered her control, pulling the emotionless void back around her. "I was hoping I wouldn't see him again," she whispered into the comforting silence. "I guess it was a good thing, because I was dreading seeing him for no reason. I didn't feel a thing."

She could almost imagine Pap's laughter.

"I didn't. I don't feel anything anymore." Sutton stared down at the wedding ring on her finger, her hand closing into a fist.

She stood, brushing the dirt from her jeans. Then she moved from room to room before coming to stand once again in the living room, where she mentally made a list of the supplies she would need to bring when she returned tomorrow.

Going to the door, she paused before opening it.

"Night, Pap. I'll be back tomorrow if the sun's shining and the creek doesn't rise." It was the same good-bye they had spoken a thousand times during her childhood when she came for her weekly visits.

Opening the door, she walked out then closed and locked it behind her before going to her car.

She had no doubt Tate was somewhere, watching. She was tempted to flip him off, but she didn't want to antagonize him. The Porters were all mean when roused. Tate's temper didn't rise as fast as his two younger brothers, but that didn't make it any less volatile.

Driving back to her hotel, she thought about how the town hadn't grown any in the eighteen years she had been away. It had two new restaurants, the only change she could see. Sutton was tempted to go into the diner for a hamburger to see if they were still as good as she remembered yet decided not to. She wasn't ready to see any of the people she knew. She still wanted time before her parents found out she was back in town.

She didn't anticipate Tate telling them. Her parents couldn't stand the Porters, and the feeling was mutual. She doubted they even talked unless they were standing in the courtroom and her father was sitting behind the bench, passing judgment on whichever Porter was unfortunate enough to have been arrested.

Her father, nicknamed 'the judge' by everyone in town, had been strict as she had grown up. Both her parents had doted on her, she was the only child. She had a childhood of being the center of her family's attention, and enjoyed it until her senior year.

That year changed her life. She had been naïve and spoiled, believing she could have anything in life she wanted. She had been wrong, so wrong, because she couldn't have the one thing she wanted most—Tate Porter.

They flirted most of her junior year. Tate had been a senior, but it was the summer she spent with Pap when they fell in love, or so she had believed.

Every day that summer, she sneaked out of Pap's house to meet Tate in the woods. He would bring a blanket, and they would lie on the grass with the trees overhead and talk for hours. Pap knew what was going on, but he didn't tell on her. Although, he would give her worried looks each time she came in the door when it was beginning to get dark.

"You know what you're doing, girl?"

"I love him, Pap."

He shook his grey head at her. "No good is going to come out of you seeing that boy. He's trash."

"Don't say that!"

"Apple don't fall far from the tree. His pa sells that pot of his to anyone who'll buy it. He's been in the pen."

"That doesn't mean Tate—"

"Yes, it does, and you know it. The boy's just like his father."

"No, he's not. He wants to leave Treepoint with me. We're going to college together."

Pap snorted in disbelief. "He'll never leave Treepoint. He graduated this year, has he made any plans for his future? Mark my words, that boy was born and bred in the mountains. It's in his blood."

"He's waiting for me to graduate so we can go to college together."

Sutton knew back then it would be useless to argue with Pap. She believed time would prove him wrong.

Her senior year started getting rocky when her parents found out she was seeing Tate. It placed a strain on their relationship, but Sutton thought they would grow to accept Tate. They never did.

Each weekend they went out, she argued with them before and after each date. When Tate's parents died, she stood beside him at their funeral, holding his hand in one of hers and Rachel's in the other. She loved Rachel, despite their age difference, like the little sister she had never had.

Tate became remote after their deaths, he became a full-time parent to his younger siblings.

He had taken a part-time job bagging groceries at the grocery store. They weren't able to spend as much time together. She was so in love, grateful for what time they could have.

By the time prom was approaching, Sutton took Rachel with her to buy her prom dress. She wanted the perfect one. She and Tate hadn't made love yet, and so they had her prom night planned out. Her girlfriend would tell her parents Sutton was spending the night with her, giving her and Tate the night to themselves. He had reserved them a room at the hotel in Jamestown so no one would see them entering the hotel in Treepoint.

Sutton was bursting with excitement when she returned home with her dress, anxious to show it to her mother. She knew as soon as she walked through the front door that something was wrong. Her parents were waiting for her with grim faces.

"I bought my dress...Do you want to see?"

"Sit down, Sutton. We need to talk," her father ordered.

Sutton laid the dress across the back of the couch before circling around to sit down nervously. She had a terrible feeling she should run upstairs and lock herself into her room; instead, she waited anxiously to hear what her parents had to say.

"Is something wrong?"

Her father stared down at her as he said, "Tate was arrested this afternoon for selling drugs."

Sutton paled, knowing how her father felt about drugs and the people who came before his bench who were charged with that crime.

"Drugs?"

"Pot," her father answered shortly.

Sutton gave a breath of relief. "If there weren't any other drugs, then that's not so bad. He—"

Her parents' expressions showed their shock at her response. Sutton turned bright red, aware of her parents' attitude toward pot.

"I know I've raised you to be respectful of the law."

"Daddy, everyone smokes it—"

"No everyone doesn't" her father had angrily cut her off. "Be quiet, Sutton. I can see we've made a terrible mistake letting you see Tate. His father was in my courtroom several times, but I wanted to give Tate the benefit of the doubt. I was wrong. He's going to follow in his father's footsteps, and I have no intention of watching my daughter lead that kind of life. How do you think you can become a lawyer if you're already looking the other way when laws aren't obeyed?"

Sutton stared silently at her father. She had received a scholarship to the University of Kentucky where she had planned to pursue a law degree. After Tate's parents' deaths, however, she intended to go to a nearby community college until Tate's brothers graduated, and could assume Rachel's care. It would take several years longer, but she was in love with him, and he was worth waiting for so they could leave Treepoint together.

"You're not to see him anymore."

Sutton stood up. "I won't do that. I love him! We're going to be together, no matter what you say!" Sutton stormed around the couch, picking up her pale coral prom dress in the expensive garment bag then going to the staircase.

"Stay away from him, or I'll make sure he loses custody of his brothers and sister." Her father's harsh order had her coming to a stop with her foot on the first step.

"You wouldn't do that!" Sutton cried out.

"Watch me! Who do you think will be hearing his case when he's brought to trial? Me. I can send him away, Sutton. I have the power to do it. If he's sent away, his brothers and sister will be put in a foster home. Do you want that to happen?"

"You wouldn't do that," Sutton whispered, shocked at the vehemence in her father's voice.

"I don't want to, but I will if you don't break it off with him."

Sutton stared at her mother pleadingly. "Mom, I love him. Please…" Tears coursed down her cheeks as her heart broke into tiny pieces.

"It's for the best, Sutton. Tate will hold you back from the future you deserve."

"Tate's going to want to know why I'm breaking up with him," Sutton argued. "I'll just wait until I'm eighteen. I can do what I want then."

Her father shook his head. "Do you really think this will be the last time Tate gets caught? Next time, I won't offer to save him. I'll just send his ass off. I suggest you make damn sure he doesn't come around you anymore. I know this hurts now, but you'll get over him after a few months."

"Please Daddy, don't make me." Sutton pled, trying to reason with her father, soon seeing it was useless.

"You're wrong. I'll never stop loving Tate. I'll never forgive you for this. I'll do what you want, but as soon as I graduate, I'm leaving, and I won't be back." With that, Sutton ran upstairs, slamming her bedroom door and locking it behind her, ignoring her father's yell as she threw herself on her bed, crying helplessly.

Burying her face in a pillow, she cried until she had no tears left. Then she rolled over and stared sightlessly up at the ceiling, knowing what she was going to have to do. Tate loved her, so she was going to have to make him believe her feelings had changed. He would hate her for this, but he would stay out of jail and keep his family intact.

Sitting up on the side of her bed, she picked up the phone on her bedside table. It took her a few phone calls to get the information she needed. Wiping the tears still clinging to her cheeks, she punched in the numbers.

"Hi, Cash." Sutton deliberately made her voice turn flirtatious. "This is Sutton. You busy?"

She heard the surprise in his voice as they talked. She tried to pretend interest, telling herself over and over it was for Tate.

After he finished talking about his last football game, Sutton brought up the reason for her call.

"Have you asked anyone to the prom yet?"

"No."

"Want to go with me?" she asked in a rush before she could change her mind.

A brief silence met her question.

"I thought you were going with Tate."

"We broke up. I really want to go, and since you've asked me out a couple of times since school started, I was wondering if you would take me."

"Okay. I think we'll have a good time." Sutton heard the insinuation in his voice.

"Me, too."

"You okay? You sound funny."

Sutton cleared her throat. "I'm fine. Just have a small cold. I'll see you at school tomorrow."

"See you then."

"Goodnight, Cash." Sutton hung up the phone, any chance she had of a future with Tate now eliminated.

CHAPTER FOUR

"Did you see anything while you were out?"

"No. Why?" Tate asked, looking up from his plate at Greer.

"You're not eating your dinner." Greer nodded at his still-full plate, and Dustin was watching him just as curiously.

"Guess I'm not hungry." Tate shoved his chair back from the table and stood up.

He went outside, staring at the mountains that surrounded his home. Leaning on the railing, he picked up a pack of cigarettes and took one out. Pulling the lighter from his pocket, he lit the tube and sucked in a deep breath.

"What's going on, Tate?" Dustin came to his side, leaning against the banister.

Tate glanced at the worried frown on his youngest brother's face. Dustin had matured fast over the last few years with the responsibility of a child. Tate was proud of the way he had stepped up to make a living for his son. Dustin had worked hard to become an accountant despite everyone not taking him seriously. He still fought an uphill battle; he had only five clients. The people in town were more worried he would steal their money than keep an accurate count. To the people in Treepoint, Porters would always be trash.

"When I went to the field, I heard a car at Pap's house." Tate kept his voice low. He didn't want Dustin worried unnecessarily for Logan's safety.

"Really? Shit. That's the first time in years anyone's been in that junk heap. Did you see who it was?"

"Sutton Creech."

Dustin gave him a sharp look. "What's she doing back in town?"

"Didn't ask. I don't imagine she'll stay long. Probably here to see that property."

"Shit. The Hayeses aren't going to be happy about that."

"No, they're not. They've been using that property for the last three years to grow their weed. They think it's funny as shit that the judge's father's land is being used to grow weed under his nose."

"Damn, you think they'll mess with her?"

"I don't know. It depends on how long she stays and if she stays away from the back part of the property. The Hayeses probably already dug up this year's supply, so she should be fine until spring. She won't be hanging around that long, anyway."

"What if she decides to sell?"

"Who's going to be stupid enough to buy it, knowing they'll have to deal with the Hayeses?"

"You going to tell her?" Dustin lifted a brow.

"Fuck no. I'm not sticking my nose where it's none of my fucking business. Asher and Holt are mean fuckers, but if Sutton doesn't go snooping, they'll leave her alone."

"What if they don't? You going to do anything?"

Tate snorted. "Sutton doesn't need me to fight her battles. She can take care of herself."

He would never forget the day Sutton showed him exactly what he meant to her. After chasing her all senior year, he saw she was spending the summer with her pap, and used the opportunity to his advantage. They saw each other all that summer, getting to know each other better.

Most of the boys in the school had chased after the beautiful girl. She had smiled at some and dated a few, ignoring the rest. He and Cash Adams were two she had ignored. The rivalry between them over the girls in town was becoming heated by that point, neither worrying about stepping on the other's toes. Looking back now, Tate realized it had been stupid and childish.

When Cash went out with a girl Tate liked, he would retaliate by going out with one Cash liked. The girls became a game to them, neither of them caring about the broken hearts they left behind...until Sutton.

He grew close to her during that summer. When she began making plans to go off to college together, he didn't tell her no, though he often changed the subject when he could. She stood beside him during the worst time of his life when his parents died. He leaned on her for help with Rachel, and she came through, helping her with her homework and holding her when Rachel would break down in tears that he didn't know how to deal with.

As her prom drew closer, he wanted to make it up to her for all the help she had given him, so he decided to make the night special for her. They hadn't made love yet, since Sutton was too shy to let him go further than kissing her other than the few times she let him brush her breast with his hand. It had been a frustrating time in his life because he was already used to girls putting out when he wanted. Sutton was refreshing and sweet, driving him insane.

He had rented a room in Jamestown, since both of them knew their relationship was going to change that night. Sutton wasn't going to walk out of that hotel the virgin she was when she went inside. He wanted to give her a taste of what the other girls at school would have with their dates renting limos. However, even with working part-time at the grocery store, he didn't have the extra money to pay for one, so he got sloppy selling a few bags of pot to several of the boys from school who wanted it for prom night.

He was driving home from work when the sheriff pulled him over. Tate hated the old bastard, but he had been smart enough to step out of his car when told to. The evil gleam in the sheriff's eye showed he was waiting for Tate to argue. It didn't take him five minutes to find the pot hidden in his car; as a result, Tate knew someone had snitched on him. He was handcuffed and taken to the sheriff's office five minutes later.

He hadn't known who to call to get him out of jail. With his parents dead, he had no relatives to turn to for help. He had called Sutton, only to have her father pick up the phone. He had been humiliated as he haltingly explained he needed to talk to Sutton. Her father had never been overly friendly with him, but he hadn't been rude, either. When the judge had told him Sutton was out shopping, Tate had become desperate, not wanting to leave his brothers and sister home alone for the night, and had told the judge he was in jail then asked for help.

Surprisingly, the judge showed up at the jail and had him released. Tate's mouth twisted bitterly at the memory. He was sickeningly grateful as they walked outside together, the sheriff watching impassively after handing him his car keys as they went out the door.

"Thank you, sir. I promise I won't do—"

"Don't make promises you aren't going to keep. You want to thank me? Stay away from Sutton," the judge had ordered.

Tate stopped walking to stare at the judge. "I can't, sir. I care about her."

"A Porter never cared about anything more than how much weed they're selling and not getting caught. Are you going to drag Sutton down like your father dragged down your mother? Is that what you want?"

"No, sir. I'm not going to sell it anymore. I just needed the money for—"

"I don't care why you needed the money this time. Every time you need it, you'll pull out your bag and sell it again. It's how you were raised. I've never known a Porter to make a living legally. It's why most of your kin's in the pen or dead. You will be, too, and I'll be damned if I'm doing to watch my daughter being dragged through the dirt with you."

Tate's hands clenched at his sides. "Sir, I appreciate your help, but I won't stop seeing Sutton."

The judge's lips tightened. "Then I guess we have nothing further to say to each other, do we?"

"No, we don't."

The judge gave him a sharp nod then got in his expensive car and drove away, leaving Tate standing in the parking lot. Tate drove home, and not wanting to get Sutton in trouble with her father, he didn't call her that night. Instead, he searched for her the next day at school when he dropped Greer and Dustin off.

Usually, she waited for him at the entrance of the school, and they would share a quick kiss before she went inside. Tate waited as long as he could before he went to work without being late.

That day went from bad to worse. When she didn't meet him after school, he knew she was mad at him. Thinking her father had told her to stay away from him, he decided he was going to drive by her house after picking Greer up from football practice. However, when he walked into the locker room, it went silent, his friends avoiding his eyes. Greer, who was changing out of his uniform, gave him a curious look.

"Did Sutton tell you she ate lunch with Cash?"

"No." Tate kept his voice low so no one could hear his reaction.

Greer nodded. "It made me fucking sick. She couldn't keep her hands off him. I sit behind him in biology, and I heard him tell Miller that Sutton asked him to the prom."

Tate slammed his fist against Gree's locker, immediately going toward Cash who was standing with his friends.

Greer tried to hold him back, but he shoved him away.

"What's up with you and my girl?" Tate snarled at Cash.

"Sutton's not your girl. She told me so herself last night."

Tate's gut churned in anger. "She's mine, so stay the fuck away from her."

"I can't do that. I'm taking her out tonight then to the prom on Saturday. If you have a problem with that, then you shouldn't have broken up with her."

"I didn't break up with her!"

"That's what she told me. Good to know she likes to stretch the truth. Of course, it's not going to keep me from going out with her, but at least I'll know not to trust her."

Tate lunged at Cash; however, the other players held him back. It wasn't that they didn't want to see the fight; they just didn't want the coach to get pissed off and make them run their asses off again.

Tate angrily shook them off going back outside to wait for Greer. He drove Greer home, instead of taking Greer's advice to move on to another pussy, he drove back into town to Sutton's home. Her mother answered the door, saying Sutton wasn't home from school yet. Tate knew the woman was lying, but he backed off, unable to do anything else except drive home where he called Sutton several times, trying to reach her. Her mother answered each time, telling him she wasn't there.

Then Tate remembered Cash saying that he and Sutton were going out that night. He ended up pacing around his house until finally going to bed.

The next day, he dragged his brothers and Rachel out of bed, determined to get to school early enough that Sutton couldn't get past him without talking to him.

He was waiting by the front school door when Cash drove up in his truck, opening the passenger door for Sutton. After putting his arm around her, she and Cash approached him.

Tate swallowed hard. He didn't have to be told; he knew. Sutton was different. The innocent, shy look in her eyes was gone, and she moved stiffly. Cash had fucked her, and Tate's world crumbled around him. He had believed Sutton's father had pressured her not to see him again. He was wrong. She had dumped him for only one reason—she wanted Cash.

Cash brought Sutton to a stop a few feet from him. "We going to have a problem?"

Tate stared at Sutton coldly, remembering how many times she had refused to let him touch her over the last few months, while Cash had managed to take her virginity after only being alone with him a few hours.

"No. You don't have a fucking thing I want anymore."

Sutton kept her gaze turned away from him, but she paled at his angry words.

"Tate, I'm sorry…" She broke off, quickly glancing at him, then away again.

"Don't be. You were nothing but a tiebreaker, anyway."

Her eyes jerked back to his. "A tiebreaker?"

Tate stared back at her mockingly. "Cash and I have each fucked eight girls the other wanted. If I had fucked you, you would have made number nine. You would have broken the tie in my favor. Congratulations, Cash, you win for now. I hear Lisa doesn't have a date for prom." Greer had told him Cash had been chasing after the dark-haired senior for the last couple of months.

"You're a fucking prick, Tate."

Cash's arm stiffened around Sutton.

Tate shrugged. "I already paid for the hotel room this Saturday, so I'm not going to let it sit empty."

Sutton's face paled further. "Let's go, Cash. I don't want to be late for class."

Tate held the door open for them, wanting to rip them apart yet too proud to let Sutton see how badly she had hurt him.

He was still standing in the doorway when he saw Lisa get out of her mother's car.

"Hey, Lisa."

"Tate."

He held the door open for her then walked with her down the hallway. He waved nonchalently to the principal, a customer with a secret habit. Sutton and Cash were both standing by Sutton's locker. He talked casually to Lisa as they came to a stop by her locker.

Feeling Sutton's eyes on them, he brushed Lisa's hair away from her cheek. "You look pretty today."

"Thanks, Tate."

They stayed at her locker, talking for several minutes, as he managed to convince her to let him go to prom with her. When the homeroom bell rang, he straightened off her locker, telling her he would meet her after school.

"You are eighteen aren't you?" He teased seductively running his tumb over her bottom lip.

"Yes." She sent him a flirtatious smile before she hurried off to her class.

He then sent a gloating look in Sutton's direction as she passed him to go to her homeroom, hardening himself against the tears he saw in her eyes and telling himself over and over what Pa always told him.

"No one hurts a Porter and gets away with it. No one."

CHAPTER FIVE

Sutton picked up a package of drop cloths, moving to the cleaning aisle in the local hardware store, hoping she would see less people in this store than the local grocery store. She would wait to go at night when she was sure not many customers would be in the store. She knew it was useless to avoid the locals who knew her, but she wanted to dodge as many as possible. She wasn't looking forward to answering any of the nosy questions she was sure would be asked of her.

Putting a gallon of bleach and a mop in her buggy, she went to the cash register where she recognized the woman ringing up purchases. Sutton ignored her curious gaze, handing her the cash for her supplies.

"Sutton Creech?" Cheryl asked in dismay.

"Hi, Cheryl."

"Damn, I can't believe my eyes. I almost didn't recognize you."

Sutton was aware of the difference in her appearance. She wasn't seventeen anymore. Overall, the years had been kind to her, although they had been better to Cheryl, who was still as attractive as she had been in high school.

"How long are you visiting?"

"I don't know yet. I haven't made up my mind." Sutton picked up her bag, wanting to get out the door as fast as possible.

"Wait, you can't just run off! We used to be best friends. Look, give me a minute, and we can go get a cup of coffee."

"I'm kind of in a hurry. Maybe next time…" Sutton felt guilty after seeing the disappointment on Cheryl's face. She remembered the many sleepovers they'd had in high school.

Sutton relented. Trying to avoid everyone was going to be a waste of time. Treepoint was too small. She would be better off just getting it over with and satisfying their curiosity. Then the town gossips could move on to someone else.

"Never mind. I'll put my bag in my car and meet you outside."

Cheryl's face broke into a smile as she motioned for some-one to take over the counter. Jared didn't look happy as Cheryl explained they were going for a break. Sutton hadn't liked Jared in high school, and she could see he hadn't changed any since he and Cheryl had been together.

Sutton went outside, placing the bag in the trunk of her car. She was slamming it shut when she saw Cheryl came outside.

"You sure you have the time to go for a coffee? Jared didn't look too happy."

Cheryl made a comical face. "I quit worrying about what Jared thought when I found out he was cheating on me." Cheryl placed her arm through hers as they walked down the sidewalk toward the diner. Sutton felt uncomfortable with the friendly gesture, so she sped up, forcing Cheryl to release her.

The restaurant was busy with the breakfast crowd when they entered, but few of the customers paid them any attention.

She and Cheryl managed to grab a small table for two in the corner and ordered coffee before the waitress could escape.

"I'm sorry to hear about Jared." Sutton immediately directed the conversation toward Cheryl. If she was still like she was in high school, it would keep them occupied until it was time to return from her break.

Cheryl shrugged. "I went a little crazy when I found out. Our divorce was just final a few weeks ago. He had the nerve to fight it after I found out he was banging five different women in town. He had even put one up in her own apartment so he could visit her anytime he wanted."

Sutton felt terrible for her friend. She knew how much Cheryl had idolized her jock boyfriend in high school.

"You warned me he was cheating on me before you left town, and I didn't listen. I should have."

Sutton's lips twisted into a wry smile. "I didn't take any of your advice, either, so we're even."

"Which one was the reason you left town? Tate or Cash?"

"Neither." Sutton leaned back in her chair so the waitress could set their coffees down. "I left for college. Anything I had with Tate and Cash was over before I packed my suitcases."

Cheryl gave a short laugh. "I couldn't believe my eyes when you showed up at prom with Cash in that green dress. You two looked like you were made for each other."

"Hardly. Cash and I never went out again after that night. He had moved on to another girl by Monday."

"Well, he's settled down now. He's married to Rachel Porter."

"I can't imagine Cash settling down with one woman."

"Believe it. Besides, how can he get away with cheating? Her brothers would kill him, and Rachel is just as good with a shotgun."

"I'm happy for them," Sutton said truthfully.

"Wish my marriage had turned out as well, but my divorce is working out much better. I quit working at the hardware store when I found out Jared was cheating on me. It was hard with him owning the store, but after the divorce, he offered me my job back. There aren't a lot of jobs around, and he promised to keep our personal life out of it. So far, it's worked out well. We're getting along better than when we were married. We've even gone out a couple of times."

Sutton narrowed her eyes at Cheryl's expression. "Be careful you don't fall down that rabbit hole twice, Alice."

She waved away her concern. "I'm not as innocent as I was in high school. After I found out Jared was cheating, I had a little payback of my own."

"Really?" Sutton couldn't imagine Cheryl taking that route.

"Really. I almost joined a biker club, but I screwed up, and they tossed me out."

"A biker club is in Treepoint?" The small town *had* changed since she left.

"Yep, and a pretty big one, too."

From the look on Cheryl's face, Sutton was sure she was more upset about losing the biker club than Jared.

"Have they been keeping the judge busy?"

"Nope. The Porters have, though. Greer was caught selling some of his weed to an undercover cop, and Tate went to court not too long ago for getting in a fight with Lyle Turner."

Sutton kept her expression neutral. "What happened?"

"With Lyle or court?"

"Both."

"Lyle towed Greer's truck when he broke down on the road home. When Tate took him to pick it up at Lyle's garage, he charged him twice the tow charge. It started an argument, but Lyle was drunk and swung first, so your father threw the case out." Cheryl's head tilted to the side. "Your dad didn't tell you any of this?"

"He must have forgotten to mention it," Sutton said evasively. She already knew much of what Cheryl had told her, since she read the *Daily Herald* online every day, but she figured, if Cheryl was gossiping about everyone else, she wasn't questioning her. Of course, no sooner did the thought pop into her head than Cheryl turned the conversation in her direction.

"Enough about me and the town. What about you?" She nodded at her hand. "Who did you marry? How long have you been married?"

"I'm a widow."

Cheryl paled, her hand reaching out to cover Sutton's on the table. "I'm so sorry."

Sutton moved her hand away, not wanting the gesture of sympathy. "Thank you. He died six years ago. I'm over the worst of it." She told the partial truth. She would never recover from Scott's death.

She reached for her purse. "You better get back to work. You've been gone for twenty minutes."

"Dammit. I'll catch you later. I'll drop by your parent's—"

"I'm not staying there. I'm staying at Pap's cabin."

"Why? No one's been there for years."

Sutton didn't miss having to explain every detail of her life.

"I wanted some rest and relaxation while I'm visiting." She stood, giving Cheryl a brief hug. "Get back to work. I'll take care of the bill. I'll see you before I leave."

"You better. I've missed you. Bye, Sutton."

"Bye, Cheryl."

Sutton went to the cash register to pay the check, ignoring the glances she felt on her back as she headed to the door. She was about to push the door open when she saw a couple sitting at one of the tables.

Tate was sitting in the restaurant with a woman she didn't recognize. She was very attractive, smiling at Tate, and a child, who looked about five or six, was seated at the table next to them. When Tate looked up, Sutton glanced away from his gaze, quickly going out the door.

The little boy had the Porter red hair. Did Tate have a child while she was gone, or was that Dustin's son? He would be about the right age from what she remembered from the news article. The *Daily Herald* had written about Samantha Langley's death and her missing child. Months later, another article had given an update of how a man named Knox had been cleared of her death and that her child had been found.

Sutton had always wondered what a child of Tate's would look like. She now had her answer. The little boy inside the restaurant was the image of him. He had the same auburn hair and green eyes. Their facial features were similar, although where Tate's features were harsh with an I-don't-give-a-fuck attitude, the little boy was all boyish innocence.

Sutton dug her fingernails into the palm of her hands, battling back emotions she had thought were locked away. She forced them back, strengthening the emotionless void that was the only way she knew to survive.

She started to cross the street as she almost bumped into a couple who were about to enter the diner. They stared at her curiously, both of them taking only a second to recognize her.

"Sutton."

"Hello, Cash…Rachel."

Of the two, Cash Adams was the friendliest. Rachel's smile had left her face, an angry glint entering her eyes.

"When did you get back in town?"

Rachel didn't wait to hear the answer to her husband's question, trying to ignore her as she headed inside the restaurant. Cash draped his arm around her shoulders, holding her in place.

Sutton licked her lips. This was far worse than she had anticipated it would be. Rachel wasn't even trying to hide her hatred.

"A couple of days ago." Sutton began to leave, not wanting Rachel to feel uncomfortable.

"Where are you staying?"

Sutton hesitated. Cash was the only one in town who knew she wouldn't be stepping into her old home.

"I've been staying at the hotel, but I'm going to be staying at Pap's house."

Cash's face became concerned. "That place has been empty for a long time. Be careful. Several of the men around town have been using it while you've been gone."

"The house or the property?"

"The property."

"If they stay away from the house, then it'll be fine."

"You have a gun?"

Sutton rolled her eyes. "What do you think?"

"Good. Keep it loaded. If you have any trouble, call Knox. He's a friend of mine and the sheriff now. I'll let him know you're staying out there and to keep an eye on you."

"Thanks, Cash." Sutton didn't look at him, keeping her eyes on Rachel's expression. The two were going to have a massive fight when she left.

"Congratulations on your marriage. I hope you both will be very happy." Sutton glanced away, her voice choking with emotion. She had known Rachel hated her, but being faced with it was hard. At one time, she and Rachel had been extremely close.

"I better be going and let you two eat your breakfast. It was nice to see you both again." Sutton moved away without giving them a chance to answer, stepping down off the sidewalk to cross the street toward her car. A horn blared as a hand reached out, grabbing her and tugging her back onto the sidewalk.

"That was close." Sutton laughed shakily, her hand still in Rachel's. She was shocked Rachel hadn't pushed her farther into the car's path.

A strange look crossed Rachel's face as Sutton tried to pull her hand back. Rachel didn't release it. Turning it over, she stared down at the palm of her hand then her wrist.

Sutton forcefully jerked her hand away, clenching her hand into a fist and dropping it to her side to hide the scars that were clearly visible.

"Bye." Sutton tried to leave again, this time watching the traffic more carefully.

"Sutton...Why don't you come to dinner this Saturday?"

She abruptly turned back to face Rachel, shocked. "I would like that."

Rachel nodded. "Cash can text you directions to our home."

"I'll look forward to it, then. Thanks for saving my life just now." Sutton waved her hand at the road.

Rachel's gaze dropped to her hand. "I'm glad I was here to help."

Sutton turned red as she stepped more cautiously into the road. She went to her car and slid inside, an uneasy feeling that Rachel had only invited her out of pity after seeing her hand and wrist foremost in her mind. It didn't matter. Hers was one expression of sympathy she wouldn't turn away from. Sutton would take anything she could get to have a chance to talk to her.

She turned her hand over on the steering wheel, staring down at the ugly scars marring them. Her nails had left permanent indentions into her palms, but it wasn't the tiny circular scars that drew attention to themselves, it was the ones on her wrists. It didn't a genius to realize they were the result of a failed suicide attempt.

Sutton started her car and pulled out into traffic cautiously.

She made no effort to hide the scars. Usually, she didn't give anyone a chance to get close enough to see them, or if they did, she refused to feel embarrassed.

Every time she looked at them, she was reminded of how she had survived and been given a second chance, a chance to right old wrongs. Rachel was the one who haunted her the most. She was the one unresolved issue Sutton needed to fix so she could move on and leave the past behind where it belonged. She wasn't the same weak, spoiled young girl who had left Treepoint behind. She was strong and could survive anything, even facing Tate and bring up all the old painful memories again. She had proved to herself that she wasn't weak anymore. This time when she left Treepoint with her goals accomplished, she wouldn't be coming back.

CHAPTER SIX

"Who's that Rachel and Cash are talking to?"

Tate dragged his eyes away from the window to answer Holly's question. "That's Sutton Creech. She used to live in town."

"Oh. Rachel doesn't seem too happy to see her," Holly remarked.

"No, she doesn't." Tate watched as his sister and her husband talked to Sutton. He was about to get up from the table, seeing how upset Rachel was, when he saw Sutton move away, nearly getting run down by a car.

Holly gasped. "I hope she's okay."

"She seems fine."

His sister's expression had changed, and Tate relaxed back against his chair. He didn't want to come into contact with Sutton any more than he had to.

A few minutes later, the couple came inside the restaurant after their conversation with Sutton ended. Tate critically surveyed his sister, trying to determine if she was upset from the encounter. When her troubled expression didn't relieve his doubts, he shot Cash an angry look, which was returned with a direct stare.

"Sorry we're late." Rachel leaned over to kiss his cheek as they took a seat at the table.

"That's okay. I saw you talking to Sutton. Are you all right?"

"I'm fine. It won't be the first or last time I run into one of Cash's old girlfriends."

"She wasn't my girlfriend. We went out a couple of times, and that was the extent of my relationship with her." Cash stared at his wife unapologetically.

Rachel took a sip of her water, avoiding her husband's gaze.

Tate wanted to ram his fist in Cash's face.

"No, she was *my* girlfriend. She was just a one-night stand to you."

Cash stiffened. "You don't know what the crap you're talking about, Tate." Cash's eyes went to Logan. Tate knew, if his nephew wasn't sitting at the table, Cash wouldn't have been so polite.

Holly threw her napkin down on the table. "Finished, Logan?" At the little boy's nod, she grabbed his hand and pulled him up from his chair before turning back to the group. "I'm going to take Logan to the library for an hour. I'll meet you back at the truck."

Holly took off with his nephew in tow, the set of her shoulders a clear reprimand. Tate stared after them, beginning to believe Greer was right. If they weren't careful, Holly would make Logan a pussy. It was time they came home. He would talk to Dustin tonight. Since they were almost finished processing the plants, there was no reason they should remain away.

"You didn't have to embarrass her, Tate," Rachel scolded.

He shrugged. "Someone has to look out for you."

Cash stiffened again. "You don't know what the fuck you're talking about. I don't have to protect Rachel from Sutton. I don't have a fucking thing to hide from her, either. There may be a lot of women I have to apologize to Rachel about, but Sutton isn't one of those women."

"Let's change the subject." Rachel placed her hand on her brother's arm. "I'm not upset, Tate."

He stared at her disbelievingly.

"It's true. I have to admit I was at first, but I'm not now. I'm not even angry at her anymore."

"Well, I am," he stated without apology.

"Tate..."

"Let's change the subject. Sutton isn't worth talking about." Tate waved his hand to catch the waitress's attention so she could take Rachel's order. He didn't give a fuck if Cash ate or not.

The waitress left after taking their order, looking relieved to get away from the tension at the table.

"She's not had an easy time since she's been gone." Rachel's soft voice didn't rouse his sympathy.

The soothing warmth he was receiving from his sister's hand on his arm didn't dispel the churning anger in his stomach, and Tate refused to talk about Sutton any longer.

Rachel sighed. "Your temper is going to be your downfall, Tate. Greer may be a hothead, but he gets over it fast. You hold a grudge forever."

"Yes, I do." He and Cash had a contentious past with fights about women, but he only remained angry about Sutton.

"You're an asshole. I never touched Sutton, but you're not going to change your mind despite me telling you the truth. Ask me about any woman in town, and I'll tell you the truth; why would I lie about her?"

"Maybe because your wife is sitting right here," Tate replied sarcastically.

"I've never denied my past to Rachel," Cash snapped back.

"Then it's because you knew I cared about her."

Cash snorted. "You didn't care about Sutton. You let her go easily enough. If you were as into her as you claim, you would have whipped my ass over her. Greer tried to give me a beating over that slut Diane. You replaced Sutton with Lisa within a day. You were just tired of having blue balls, and it gave you the excuse to do what you wanted to do all along."

"Which was what?" Tate snarled.

"Break up with Sutton and fuck Lisa. I saw her flirting with you when you would pick Greer up from football practice. Was that short little cheerleader skirt getting to you?

Tate stood, his chair scraping the linoleum. "I've gotta go before I knock the shit out of you. I can't afford to do any jail time right now. Bye, Rach."

"Tate!"

He ignored his sister trying to call him back. He didn't bother paying his bill either, knowing Cash would take care of it. The son of a bitch deserved to pay his tab.

He strode to his truck and climbed inside to wait for Holly and Logan. He slammed his hand down on the steering wheel, wanting to vent the anger he couldn't take out on Cash.

He was angry at himself and Cash. He should have beaten the ever-loving shit out of Cash all those years ago.

Tate ran his hand through his hair. He had never been with a girl as long as Sutton, certainly not one he hadn't fucked on a regular basis and remained faithful. She had made plans for their future together, despite him constantly evading the issue. He had no intention of leaving Treepoint, and he had selfishy hoped deep down that she would change her mind about leaving. Moreover, she had stood beside him when his parents died, and Rachel had grown attached to her. She'd had dreams of being a lawyer, while his dreams had been simplier—a woman who would fuck his brains out and help him raise his brothers and sister. If she could do that, he would be content never to leave his mountain.

In his mind, he had seen Sutton getting out of Cash's truck, and his pride had been stung. Truthfully, it still was. Now he realized how selfish he was being; she had only been seventeen, and he had been her first boyfriend.

Sutton had been the best part in the shit hole his life had become. She deserved to leave Treepoint and follow her dreams without him holding her back. She had probably figured that out for herself, which was why she had cheated on him with Cash.

Seeing Holly crossing the street with Logan, he got out to hold the door open for her, watching with a smile as Logan climbed inside. He ruffled the boy's red hair when he succeeded.

"I did it all by myself," Logan boasted.

"Yes, you did." Tate chuckled as Logan sat down in his carseat.

"I'm getting too big for this. Can't I just sit on the seat like you?" he complained, buckling himself in with nimble fingers.

"You have to gain a few more pounds for that to happen." Seeing the frown of discontent, Tate winked at Holly. "How about we go to the store and see if we can find the next size up? If Holly tells me you've been good at your grandmother's, I might even buy you that new bike you've been wanting."

"I've been really good, haven't I, Holly?" Logan looked anxiously at the woman sitting in the front seat.

"Yes, you have," she said, throwing Tate a furtive look.

When he was back in the truck, Holly lowered her voice. "I thought we couldn't afford it right now."

Tate shrugged. "Came into some extra money."

"I don't know how I feel about you using your drug money to buy him a bike."

Tate's mouth firmed. "It's a good thing it's not up to you then, is it?"

Holly crossed her arms over her chest, turning to stare out the window.

Tate drove them to the store, letting Logan pick out his bike after they found a booster seat for the truck. Tate ignored Holly's disapproval.

"Holly?" Logan's face fell when she didn't return his excitement.

Her expression softened as it always did where Logan was concerned. "It's a nice bike."

His excitement returned as they wheeled it toward the cash register. Tate ignored Holly's holier-than-shit attitude as he paid for the purchases. He felt no guilt over how he and his brothers earned their money. If they didn't purchase the weed from them, their customers would buy it off someone else. The money was better off in his wallet than the Hayes's or the Coleman's, and their clients damn sure were better off not smoking the weed they sold.

As they were going out the door, Tate saw Lyle Turner, the town drunk, coming in and throwing him a glare, which Tate forced himself to brush off. The case had been thrown out of court. If Lyle wanted to start a fight, he could do it with the store cameras on him. Tate wasn't about to spend a night away from home with the sense of danger he had felt lately.

Tate loaded Logan's bike into the bed of the truck and switched out the car seats before he climbed in. Logan fidgeted with excitement on the way to his grandmother's house.

"How much longer are we going to have to stay with Mrs. Langley?" Holly asked.

"Just a few more days." Tate took his eyes briefly off the road. "I figured you would prefer Mrs. Langley's house over ours. It's a hell of a lot bigger."

"It's not home." Holly glanced away, avoiding his gaze.

"It won't be much longer," Tate promised as he pulled into the driveway.

Tate climbed out while Holly opened the back door to let Logan out. The anxious boy could hardly wait as Tate pulled his bike out of the truck.

He stayed and watched him for an hour until Dustin showed. Then Tate left them alone for some private time.

Logan and Dustin had developed a close relationship, but Tate noticed an expression of sadness appear in his brother's eyes when he wasn't aware someone was watching. His young, devil-may-care attitude hid the pain Samantha had left behind. Dustin had loved her. He had never discussed it with him or Greer, but both brothers felt Dustin's pain.

Their father had warned them when they each turned sixteen that a Porter loves only once. He had often told them how he managed to catch their mother. He had loved her on first sight. Tate still remembered rolling his eyes when his father regaled them with his past. His mother had been engaged to Cash Adam's father at the time.

"I knew she was meant for me the first time I set eyes on her."

"She belonged to someone else," Tate had reminded him.

His father had shrugged. "I knew Mattie would catch on to him cheating on her. Your momma ain't nobody's fool."

"She caught him?" Greer had asked.

Their father had nodded, not trying to hide the triumph in his voice. "Kind of hard not to when he knocked up the town whore. Took me a year to talk her into going out with me, then another six months to get her in my bed."

"Ew," Dustin had groaned, covering his hands with his ears.

"Son, you won't be thinking that in a few years when a pretty girl walks by you, sashaying a pretty ass in front of you."

Tate and Greer had both laughed as their father had shot them a know-it-all grin.

"I wouldn't laugh too hard if I were you two, either. I'm gonna give you the same warning my pa gave me: once a woman catches a Porter man's heart, she never lets it go. My pa and each man before him only loved one woman."

"Not in this day and time," Tate had snickered.

He had shaken his head. "Porter men are different."

"You really believe that?" Tate had asked in disbelief.

"I know that," he had said in conviction. "I wouldn't want to live without your ma."

Tate had a feeling of forboding and quickly changed the subject. "Maybe it will skip our generation."

"I hope not. I wouldn't want you to miss out on what me and your ma have."

"Didn't Cash's dad try to get her back?"

A familiar look that had always scared them shitless had come over his face, the same one that had been on his face when he had caught someone snooping around their property.

"He tried, hard."

"What did you do?" Dustin had asked the question they all had wanted answered.

"I followed the rules my father gave me and the same one I keep telling you. A Porter always stands his ground. Don't leave an enemy standing, and always keep what's yours."

All of them had stared at their father in awe.

"Don't forget them rules," he had ordered.

"We won't." Each of them had given their promise to their father.

"When I'm dead and gone, live and breathe them. Mark my words, no man or woman will stand a chance against you."

CHAPTER SEVEN

"Dammit." Sutton stretched her aching back as she carried another box to place with the others the town church was picking up for their store. There wasn't much left of Pap's life, but she couldn't bear to trash what there was. Maybe the items could find a new home with someone who would benefit from them.

She decided to finish the rest in the morning. Going to the kitchen, which she had spent the majority of the morning cleaning, she poured herself a glass of iced tea. Not hungry, she carried it outside and stood on the porch, enjoying the cool breeze and fresh air. At least the small house no longer smelled musty.

Sutton listened as the wind rustled the tree limbs. When she was younger, the sound would have frightened her. Now it only made her search the shadows of the woods, unafraid.

The years since then had taught her it wasn't the things you couldn't see, but the evil lurking right in front of your eyes that was the more deadly. To fear danger, you had to be afraid of dying, and Sutton wasn't afraid of dying. She had courted it at one time until the medication that had been forced on her had given her mind a chance to heal. She realized then; if she was going to be forced to live this life, she was going to make it worthwhile.

Looking down at her watch, she went in to shower, dressing in a comfortable blue dress that fell just above her knees. She brushed out her hair then slid on her shoes before grabbing her purse and going outside. She didn't have to look at the directions Cash had sent her. She had looked at them several times already.

She was nervous, not wanting to cause any conflict between the husband and wife. She chewed on her bottom lip nervously as she turned down the road toward their house. There weren't any other houses down the dark road that practically ended at their front door.

Not giving herself time to change her mind, she got out of the car, picking up the gift she had brought, not wanting to take the chance she would forget it at the last minute.

At the door, Cash opened it before she could knock.

"Hi, Sutton."

"Cash." She returned his greeting, looking past him in search of Rachel.

"She's in the kitchen," Cash answered, giving her a gentle smile.

Sutton entered the cozy home, handing the bottle of wine to Cash.

"It needs to be chilled."

"I'll take care of it. Take a seat."

Sutton sat down on the dark brown leather couch, perching on the end of the cushion.

"Can I get you something to drink?"

"An iced tea, if you have it."

"Be right back." Cash disappeared as she stared around the home, taking in the pictures of Rachel and Cash that were sitting on the small end table next to the couch. The couple was obviously very much in love, and Sutton was happy for both of them.

Hearing a noise, she looked over her shoulder to see Rachel carrying a glass and Cash following behind his wife.

"Sutton, I'm glad you came."

Sutton stared at Rachel, seeing she was telling the truth. Her warm greeting dispelled some of her nervousness.

"Thank you," she said, taking the drink from Rachel.

Rachel sat down on the chair in front of the couch, and Cash sat down on the arm of the chair, his arm across the back. The closeness between the couple twisted a knife in her heart.

Taking a drink of her tea, she listened as Rachel thanked her again for the donation she was making to the church store.

"It's really not a big deal." Sutton shrugged. "I'm sure a lot of it would be better off in the trash, but I thought it would be easier for you to do than me."

"I'm sure we'll manage to use most of it," Rachel assured her.

"I hope so. Pap loved Treepoint, so I'd like to know a little of him is spread around town."

"I'll see what I can do. Most of our donated items do get taken. The only items we're finding it hard to get rid of are the ones Mag—Cash's grandmother—donated to make room for the new stuff she buys."

Cash snorted. "There's nothing new about that junk she buys at those yard sales she's addicted to."

"I'm afraid he's right. She donated a stuffed owl last month, and I swear it's the ugliest thing I've ever seen. We had to put it out back. The kids are all afraid of it."

Sutton relaxed back against the couch. "I don't have anything that bad to donate."

"Good. That thing gives me the willies every time I go to the storage room."

"Why don't you just throw it away?"

"I'm too afraid Mag will ask what happened to it."

Sutton understood. She remembered Cash's grandmother well. The woman was terrifying, a cantankerous woman who made everyone dread running into her. She could cut you to the quick with her remarks. She wasn't the sweet, grandmotherly type; she was an outspoken woman who made no attempt to filter what came out of her mouth, whether or not the recipient wanted to hear her opinion.

"How is your grandmother doing?"

"Mean as ever, but she's playing nice right now." Cash's eyes twinkled. "I've threatened to not let her great-grandchild around her if she doesn't behave."

"You're pregnant?" Sutton asked, glancing back and forth between the two.

Rachel nodded, taking Cash's hand in hers. "We just found out a couple of weeks ago."

"Congratulations," she said sincerely. At one time, hearing of someone's pregnancy would have wounded her. Now all Sutton felt was happiness that the couple was going to experience one of life's greatest joys.

"Thank you." Rachel stood up, releasing Cash's hand. "Let's eat before dinner gets cold."

They moved to the dining room where Sutton sat down in a chair at the table Rachel had obviously taken pains to set.

When she had first started dating Tate, Rachel had been self-conscious about the difference between their two families. Sutton's family was one of the wealthiest in Treepoint, whereas Rachel's was one of the poorest. Sutton had made the mistake of inviting Rachel and her brothers to dinner at her home one time, and her mother and father had looked down on them.

"It looks beautiful," Sutton complimented, appreciating the fresh flowers sitting on the middle of the table.

"Thank you. I'll just be a minute."

"Do you need any help?" Sutton started to rise from her chair.

"I have it under control. Stay and keep Cash company."

Sutton sank back down into her chair as Rachel left to go into the kitchen. She didn't try to break the strained silence that followed.

"You're looking good, Sutton."

"Thank you." She began playing with her fork. "You do, too. Marriage agrees with you."

"I've never been happier in my life."

"It shows."

"You?"

Sutton gazed directly back into his eyes. "I'm in a good place."

"That's good to hear. How long are you staying in town?"

"I haven't decided." Sutton shrugged. "Not long. I want to finish cleaning out Pap's house and then decide if I want to sell or not."

"Houses in Treepoint aren't exactly selling right now, and some people in town won't want to buy what they're already getting for free," Cash hinted. "Some could even get angry."

"I didn't care about being popular, even in high school." Her eyes darkened with memories as she remembered the cruel gossip that her so-called friends had participated in after her breakup with Tate.

"You could always set the record straight."

"Why would I do that? It didn't matter then, and it doesn't now," Sutton stated matter-of-factly.

"Don't sit there and fucking lie to me about the gossip not hurting you. I tried to tell everyone I didn't touch you, but with my reputation, no one would believe me. You didn't even try to defend yourself."

"What would have been the point? They wouldn't have believed me either, not after Tate saw us together that morning."

"You could have told him that you got into an argument with your dad when I came to pick you up and fell down your steps. You almost broke your damn neck, and would have, if I hadn't managed to catch you before you hit the landing. You were bruised. You could have shown Tate. You could have made him believe you if you had wanted to, Sutton. Why didn't you?"

"Have you ever heard the saying, 'If you love something, set it free, if it comes back to you, it's yours; if it doesn't, it never was'?"

"Shit. You were testing Tate, and he failed, didn't he?"

"It wasn't a test, Cash. I knew I was putting too much pressure on Tate. He had the responsibility of his brothers and Rachel, but I loved him so much I couldn't help myself. You heard the argument between me and my dad. He would have made sure Tate went to jail when he went to court."

"So you were keeping Tate out of trouble and giving him time to come to a decision about your relationship?"

"Yes. I knew when I did it that I was taking a chance I would lose him," Sutton said softly as she stared down at the table, lost in the past.

"Tate was a dumb fuck then, and he's not changed." Cash's voice was laced with fury.

"This is one time I won't disagree with you," Rachel said angrily.

Sutton's eyes jerked to the doorway. She had been so lost in the past that she hadn't seen Rachel reenter, carrying a platter of grilled steaks.

It was now or never. Sutton wanted Rachel to know the truth.

"I was going to talk to you later in the evening. I always felt guilty about leaving you, Rachel. I felt like you were my little sister, and I didn't want you still hating me after all this time. Life is too short, and I wanted to make sure you knew that, when Tate and I broke up, it wasn't a betrayal of our friendship."

Rachel set the platter of steaks on the table before coming to stand next to her chair. "I was so angry at you, but I missed you, Sutton, so badly." Tears glistened in Rachel's eyes. "Every time

I saw my friends, who are sisters, together, it would make my missing you worse. Then I would resent you for not being there."

"I'm sorry, Rachel. I really am."

Rachel nodded. "I believe you."

Sutton stood up from the table. "I've missed you just as much. I came into town and saw you graduate. I even saw you get married," Sutton confessed. "Cash called and told me he was hoping for a shotgun wedding. I sat in the back of the church." She laughed. "No one even noticed I was there with the spectacle your brothers made."

Rachel winced. "Don't remind me." She reached out, giving her a hug. "I'm glad you're back, Sutton. I hope you stay long enough for us to become friends again."

Sutton hugged her back. "I'd like that."

Rachel released her. "Good. Now let's eat before the food gets any colder."

As they ate, Rachel told her about working for The Last Riders. Sutton was surprised a motorcycle club actually ran a legitimate company. What didn't come as a surprise was that Cash was a member.

"I bet that gave all the gossips something to talk about for a while."

"Most of the town was afraid of them when they first came to town, but now they're pretty much accepted by everyone."

"I wouldn't go that far," Cash countered.

"Well...not *as* afraid. I'll have to set up a lunch with my friends to introduce you to them. Do you remember Lily and Beth Cornett? They're married to two of the members. Winter Simmons is, too. She was one of the teachers before she became principal."

Sutton ate as she listened to Rachel, dreading when the topic of conversation would turn to her. She had taken a bite of apple pie when the unavoidable happened.

"So, what have you been up to since you left high school?"

She swallowed her bite of dessert before answering with the rehearsed reply. "I went to college and graduated. I work in pharmaceutical sales and then volunteer part-time to help people who are sick and can't afford the medicine my company sells."

"I thought you wanted to be a lawyer."

"I changed my mind," Sutton said abruptly.

"I didn't…" Rachel looked at her intently. "I'm sure it's very fulfilling for you to help others in need."

"It is," Sutton agreed, setting down her glass of tea.

"What charity is it? Perhaps Cash and I—"

She shook her head. "I didn't come here to get donations, Rachel."

Both Cash and Rachel stared at her, and Sutton bit her bottom lip.

"Why don't you tell me what you do want from me?" Rachel asked.

Cash's hard face stared back at her. She could tell he was very protective of his wife and the child she was carrying. Suddenly, she knew it was wrong of her to ask Rachel for her help.

Sutton stood up. "Nothing. I just wanted to clear up any hard feelings between us. I better be going. It's getting late. Thanks for dinner. Night, Cash, Rachel."

Before they could say anything, she rushed out the door and onto the front porch.

"Sutton! Wait!"

Sutton turned at Rachel's voice, keeping her face impassive as Rachel came out farther onto the porch, closing the door behind her.

"Let me help, Sutton. Please don't run away again. It doesn't solve anything. Believe me, I know."

Sutton shook her head vehemently. "You can't help me."

"Maybe I can. You remember I can heal. You saw me do it when I was younger. It's become stronger as I grew older."

"You can't help." She waved her hand at Rachel's abdomen. "Besides, I saw what it did to you after you helped someone, and you're carrying a baby. I won't let you endanger yourself or Cash's child. Let it go. It wasn't important, anyway." Sutton turned, about to step off the porch.

"I think it is. I think it's the most important thing in the world to you."

Sutton didn't turn back to face Rachel, too afraid she would see the truth on her face.

"You've tried to take your life. Whatever is wrong isn't just going to disappear."

"You can't fix me. No one can." She slowly turned back to face the only person left in this world she felt any emotion for.

"No, but I can ease the pain. That's why you're here, isn't it?"

"Yes...or..."

"*Or?*"

"To say good-bye."

CHAPTER EIGHT

"This is bullshit." Tate turned to his lawyer who was sitting next to him. "I didn't say one word to Lyle when I passed him at the store."

"I don't understand it, either." Diamond's low voice made him aware his own loud one was drawing everyone's attention in the packed courtroom. "Knox tried to talk Lyle out of filing the complaint, but he wouldn't listen. Even Rachel asked Jo to reason with him, but she was just as unsuccessful. She says, over the last few months, he's been drinking more and more."

"That isn't all he's doing more of." Tate cast Lyle a glance. The town drunk was sitting somewhat soberly in the front-row seats.

"All rise." The bailiff's words had Tate getting to his feet as Judge Creech entered the courtroom from the side door. He was shocked at the judge's appearance. Tate had thought the judge wasn't aging well the last time he had been in court, but this time, he knew it for a fact. The man looked pale and haggard, as if he didn't know what a good night's sleep was anymore.

The bailiff read the complaint against him, his eyes focused on the papers in his hands.

"Did Mr. Porter try to make any attempt to approach you, Mr. Turner? Keep in mind that I can ask for the video to be played."

"Yes, sir. That's what I understand."

Tate almost snorted out loud. The man's brain was too fried on that synethetic weed to comphrehend exactly what had happened. The large amounts of synthetic weed and alcohol he was mixing were a deadly combination. The lawyer whispering in Lyle's ear must be clueing him in to the penalties for perjury.

"If Mr. Porter did, in fact, threaten you, then it should make no difference if it was recorded by store surveillance."

Tate raised a brow, not at the stern tone the judge was using, but the direction the questioning was going. He had expected to be given a couple of days in jail despite not being guilty of confronting Lyle.

"Would you like to drop the complaint before I ask the bailiff to play the tape?"

Lyle's face turned a bright red as he glared at him. "Yeah."

"Case dismissed." Judge Creech raised his gavel and slammed it down on the sound block.

Diamond rose, turning to him and smiling. "That worked out well. I might not even charge you this time."

Tate opened his mouth, but before he could say anything, she changed her mind.

"Of course, that wouldn't be good business."

"I've been giving you enough business lately. You should let this one be a freebie."

"I would, but there is a new pair of heels I'm dying to buy." She picked up her briefcase. "Maybe next time."

Tate watched as his lawyer left the courtroom. He was sure she would be able to buy several pairs of those expensive shoes she liked to wear on the fees she charged him.

Lyle gave him a smug-ass grin as he asked the bailiff to escort him out of the courtroom. Tate's hands clenched at his side. If he wasn't sure he would be forking over another fee to Diamond to buy matching purses, he would kick Lyle's ass.

"Tate."

He turned to see Judge Creech motioning to him from a doorway at the side of his bench. Surprised, he followed the judge through the door and down a small hallway to his office.

The judge closed the door behind them. Then he took off his robe, throwing it over a chair next to his large, wooden desk before taking a seat. Opening the drawer, he pulled out a whiskey bottle and poured himself a drink.

"You need to give Lyle a wide berth, or you're going to find yourself in jail again."

Since when did the judge offer anyone advice, much less him?

"I've been trying to do that, but in a town the size of Treepoint, it's kind of hard to do."

The judge lifted the whiskey glass, draining it before pouring himself another. "Try harder."

"Since when do you give a fuck what I do?"

Judge Creech leaned back in his chair, gazing down into his glass. "I don't." He swallowed his second drink then set his glass down on the table before staring up at him.

"Have you seen Sutton since she's been back in town?"

"Is that what this is all about? Are you worried Sutton and I will start something again?" Tate snorted. "I don't fuck married women."

Tate refused to feel guilty when the older man's face whitened at his choice of words.

"Her husband has been dead for six years."

Tate hid his surprise by shrugging. "It still doesn't matter. Your daughter broke up with me, remember?"

"How could I forget?"

Tate didn't understand the expression that crossed the judge's face. It was a mix of agony and regret.

"If you do see her again, tell her that her mother isn't doing well and would like to see her."

He didn't know how to reply, stunned that he was asked to pass along a message to Sutton when all they had to do was pick up the phone.

"Why don't you call her and tell her yourself?"

"Sutton hasn't talked to her mother or I since she graduated high school."

Shocked by the judge telling him his family's problems, it took Tate a minute to realize the man was waiting for an answer.

"I only saw her for a few minutes when she was at Pap's house. We didn't exactly spend any time shootin' the shit. It was more 'hi and bye', which is the way both of us want to keep it. What Sutton and I had ended when she cheated on me with Cash."

"Sutton never cheated on you. She's not capable of cheating on anyone she loves."

"Really?" Tate said mockingly. "Then who got out of Cash's truck the day I saw them together. It sure fucking looked like Sutton."

The man's shoulders slumped. The confident judge Tate had known for years was replaced by a man who seemed twice his age with regret shining from his eyes.

"Sutton didn't cheat on you, but I guess it doesn't matter to you now any more than it did back then." Judge Creech waved his hand toward his door. "Try to stay out of trouble, Tate. I'm retiring next month, and the next judge won't be as lenient with you as I have been."

"When the fuck were you ever lenient with me?"

"Ask that lawyer of yours. I could have made sure Rachel and those asshole brothers were taken away from you years ago. When did you ever hear about a known drug dealer keeping custody of kids? Greer could have been given a couple of years for selling to that undercover cop and planting evidence when Knox was accused for the murder of Samantha Langley. And, your ass should have been sitting in jail for six months when you assaulted Lyle."

"If that's true, then why cut me some slack when you hate me? You made that plain enough when I was dating Sutton."

"If you're so fucking smart, why don't you figure it out?"

Tate frowned. "You did it because of Sutton?"

"Now you're using that brain your mama gave you. Why don't you go home and smoke some of that weed you're so proud of and think on it a while."

The judge placed his bottle of whiskey back in the drawer with the glass before standing up and walking toward the door.

"Why are you telling me this now? Sutton and I were over a long time ago."

The judge opened the door before turning back to him. "You didn't deserve Sutton then, and you still don't. I wanted a man who would give his life for her, protect and love my baby girl the way her mother and I did. I kept waiting for you to prove me wrong. I *wanted* you to prove me wrong." He shook his head at him. "You're too big an asshole to realize what you let go, though. God help you when you do."

The man left him speechless. He was tempted to go to Sutton and ask her what the hell her father was talking about, but truthfully, he didn't want to know. No good ever came from dredging up the past. Like a coon dog, it was better to let the fuckers sleep. When you woke one up, the bastards never shut up. They could keep you awake for hours before they quieted down, and he had lost enough sleep over Sutton already.

⁎ ⁎

Sutton pushed the broom under Pap's bed, sweeping several huge dust bunnies out along with am old shoebox. She stared down at the box, recognizing it instantly. Bending over, she set it on the bed then returned to cleaning under the bed. She grabbed the dustpan, sweeping the huge pile up and tossing it into the trash can in the kitchen.

She went to the refrigerator, taking out a cold beer and popping the top. She took a long drink before going back into the bedroom and picking up the box, tucking it under her arm. Carrying the box and beer to the front porch, she sat down on the rocking chair, propping her feet onto the porch rail. She drank half the beer before she took the top off the box and stared at the myriad photos taken the summer she had been with Tate.

Taking another swallow of her beer, she picked up the first photo, gazing down into Tate's roughly hewn features. He was wearing the straw hat she hated. Shirtless and covered in sweat, he had stood, braced against the same porch rail that her feet rested on now.

She still remembered that day. They had walked through the woods from his house. He had stopped halfway to her house, pulling her close for their first kiss. The unexpected passion he had raised in her had frightened her into breaking away from him. Then she had run the rest of the way back to Pap's house. Tate had chased after her, his laughter following her.

He hadn't changed much from his picture other than a few lines at the corners of his eyes, and his body had become more muscular. The biggest difference was his eyes. The man she had seen the other day showed no mercy.

Sutton dropped the picture back into the box, picking up another one. In this one, they were lying on a quilt under a huge oak tree. She was on her back, staring up into his face. Tate was lying next to her as they stared at each other. The truth of their relationship was caught in that moment by Rachel who had caught them off-guard, taking the picture.

Her face was filled with a mixture of love and need, baring her soul. Tate's expression was just as telling. She had just been too innocent to recognize it for what it was—passion and want. His was missing the deeper emotions so easily read on hers.

Sutton crushed the photo in her hand before returning it to the old shoebox and putting the lid back on top. Then she lifted the beer bottle to her lips and was staring blindly into the dark woods, lost in the past, when a crack of gunfire filled the night.

Sutton's feet dropped to the wooden porch as she jumped up, listening as another shot rang out. She then ran inside the house, picking up her cell phone and calling 911.

The emergency operator sounded tired when she came on the line. "911, what is your emergency?"

"This is Sutton Creech. I live at 540 South Benson Road. I was outside and heard gunshots."

"Is there a victim?"

"I don't know. All I heard was gunfire."

"We'll send a patrol car out and a deputy to take your statement."

"Thank you."

After the operator disconnected the call, Sutton went to her front door, which she had left open, closing it and slamming the lock in place. She hadn't heard another shot, so to calm her taut nerves, she told herself it was probably Tate or one of his brothers out hunting.

She stood there, looking out her front window, until she saw a police car pull up outside her house with its blue lights flashing. Sutton watched a huge man get out of the sheriff's car. His size alone was reassuring enough for her to unlock and open the door before he was able to reach the front porch.

"Ms. Creech?" the sheriff asked.

"Yes."

"I'm Knox Bates. The dispatcher said you heard shots. Any idea which direction they came from?"

Sutton pointed to the woods that led down to the road into town. The sheriff pressed a button on the radio on his shoulder, sending a deputy to the direction she had pointed.

"Thanks for your help. Go inside and lock your doors." Sheriff Bates turned to leave.

"That's it?" Sutton questioned, thinking he would at least take down a statement.

"Pretty much. You told the dispatcher you didn't see anything. Is that correct?"

"Yes, I only heard two shots."

"Then there isn't any more information you can give me. My time is better spent trying to find where the shots came from. Don't you agree?" The huge man raised a questioning brow at her.

Sutton blew out an aggravated breath. "Yes."

"Go inside and lock your door. Let me and my deputy do our jobs."

She went inside her house, shutting the door behind her and locking it again. She stared out the window as the sheriff pulled out of her gravel driveway then dropped the curtain to hide the inky darkness that had her regretting her decision to stay alone at Pap's house.

She needed her head examined. She knew from the stories Pap had told her that these mountains were dangerous. Tate had made no effort to hide the danger the summer they had been together. With the property left vacant for so many years, it was just another mistake in a long line she had made.

First thing in the morning, she would go into town and contact a realtor. She would sell the house as quickly as possible and go back to California. Then the only problem she would have left would be to figure out where home was.

CHAPTER NINE

"Did you hear they found Lyle Turner dead? He was shot in the back of his head a half mile from your house."

Sutton almost dropped the Styrofoam coffee cup in her hand. She had stopped in at the diner to buy herself a cup to help wake up and had passed Cheryl in the parking lot as she was leaving.

"No, I hadn't heard." Sutton didn't tell her she had called the police when she had heard the shots last night.

"It's all people are talking about when they come into the hardware store. The sheriff is looking for Tate."

Sutton frowned. "Why Tate?"

"Lyle and Tate have had some bad blood between them lately. Lyle had a protection order against Tate. It only makes sense that he's the one who shot Lyle."

"Not to me," Sutton snapped back. "Tate might be a jerk, but he wouldn't shoot anyone in the back of the head. He wouldn't hesitate to shoot them between the eyes, but Tate wouldn't shoot anyone without giving them a chance to defend themselves."

Cheryl shrugged. "I'm just repeating what everyone is saying."

"Then everyone is wrong." Sutton opened her car door, getting inside.

"Wait, are you mad at me?" Cheryl placed her hand on the car door, preventing her from closing it.

Sutton sighed. She didn't know why she was taking up for Tate, anyway. He didn't need her to protect him. He hadn't in the past and certainly didn't need it now.

"No, I'm sorry. I guess I'm a little freaked out finding out someone was killed not far from my house."

"Oh." Cheryl's smile of relief filled her face. "That's fine. I shouldn't be repeating gossip. I hated it when I was the one everyone in town was talking about. Want to go out for a drink Friday night? I don't have many friends left in town since I alienated most of them when Jared and I were going through our divorce."

"I'd like that. Seven o'clock at that new restaurant?"

"King's?" Sutton nodded. "Sounds good. I'll meet you there."

"Bye, Cheryl."

"Bye."

Sutton closed her car door as Cheryl moved away, going inside the diner. Sutton was sure she would find someone else to talk to who would be more interested in spreading the gossip about Tate. In the meantime, it was only a couple of miles to the realtor's office.

Hall Realty was the only realty company in town. When she had looked it up online, she had realized she knew the owner of the business since Drake Hall had attended high school with her. Sutton missed the anonymity of a larger city. In Treepoint, everyone knew everyone and who your parents were, going back generations.

Cheryl knocked on the office door before hearing a brusque male voice telling her to come inside.

Drake Hall rose from behind his desk as she entered. He was powerfully built with the same smile she remembered from high school. He had been one of the handsomest boys in school, and she was sure he was still one of the best-looking men in town.

Sutton introduced herself, taking the hand he held out.

"Judge Creech's daughter?"

"Yes."

"I haven't seen you in Treepoint for years."

"I live in San Diego now. I want to sell the house my grand-father left me."

Drake's smile slipped for a brief second as he waved her to a chair in front of his desk before returning to his own. "Property isn't exactly selling right now. What kind of condition is the house in?"

"I'm cleaning it, and I'm going to put in a new kitchen and bathroom before we place it on the market. It should only take a couple of weeks. I've already contacted a contractor."

"I see."

"I thought the improvements would help it sell?" Sutton inquired, seeing the heavy frown on Drake's face.

"Usually, it does, but in your case, I don't think it's going to make much of a difference. I don't know how you're set finan-cially, and I would hate to see you wasting your money on a house that's going to take time to sell."

"Why won't it make a difference?"

"Because anyone who buys that house will be buying it for the land."

Sutton silently agreed with his assessment.

"I'm aware someone is using it to grow their weed," she broached the subject they were both skirting around.

"Then you know the only one who's going to buy it is the one using it to farm their crops. They won't step forward, because they probably don't have the money and won't want to make it known they're using the land, and no one else will buy it, afraid of pissing someone off who's already using the land for free."

Sutton sighed. "I was afraid of that. I still want to put it on the market. Maybe, if the price is right, someone will be tempted to take on whoever's been using my land illegally."

"The only ones I can think of who might be willing to buy that stretch of land are the Porters. They're strong and mean enough to handle whoever it is, and they certainly won't care about who it will piss off."

"I agree. If not, then some other buyer may come forward. Would you be interested in helping me sell my grandfather's home?"

He gave her an assured smile. "I never turn down money. I'll do the paperwork and stop by your house later this week to take pictures to put online."

"That works for me. Thank you." Sutton rose from her chair.

Drake stood, putting his hand out. "It was good seeing you again, Sutton."

"You, too." She released his hand after shaking it, relieved to escape his office. The man had become even more sexually attractive than he had been in high school.

Back then, he'd had a steady girlfriend. From the absence of a wedding ring on his finger, Sutton surmised he wasn't married, and she wasn't anxious to spend any time alone with the man. She wasn't the innocent girl who didn't recognize a man who was obviously used to playing the field. She had been down that road twice in her life, and she wasn't stupid enough to travel it again. Twice was already more than enough. One had left her heartbroken, and the second had nearly killed her.

Sutton stopped to pick up a few groceries before driving home, relieved the store hadn't been busy and she hadn't come face-to-face with any old acquaintances.

As she drove home, she passed several police cars. They must have been searching the back roads for Tate. She also noticed one pull out of Tate's driveway.

She flipped on her blinker, turning onto the private driveway that led to Pap's home. If she made many more trips to town, she was going to have to trade her rental car in for an SUV. Instead of updating the kitchen, she would probably do better paving the gravel driveway.

She parked the car next to the house to make it easier to pack in the groceries. Grabbing several bags, she carried them to the door, tugging the keys from out of her jean pocket. When she went to slide the key into the lock, the door came open a few inches.

Sutton swallowed the fear in her throat. She was sure she had locked her door before she had left that morning. Her eyes caught on a single drop of blood on the door handle. She started to take a step back, only to freeze when she felt someone's chest against her back. Terror let a small scream escape when she felt herself shoved forward into the house.

"Shut up. I don't know how many cops are still in the woods, searching for me." Tate's harsh voice sent relief flooding through her.

She angrily jerked around to face him, ready to blast him for scaring the hell out of her. However, the angry retort she was about to yell at him died on her lips when she saw the condition he was in.

"What happened to you?"

Tate grimaced, picking up a dish towel she had left laying on the counter. "I was stabbed."

"By whom?"

"Beats the shit out of me. When I heard someone shooting last night, I went to see what was going on, and I found Lyle with the back of his head blown off. When I tried to call Knox, someone knocked me out. When I came to, I had a knife in my chest and was lying next to Lyle with a shotgun in my hand I didn't recognize, and mine was gone, so I got the hell out of there as fast as I could."

Tate leaned heavily against the counter, his hand leaving a bloody palm print.

"Why didn't you stay and tell the sheriff?"

Tate gave her a look that plainly said he doubted her intelligence. "I don't know. Maybe it was because that fucker had a restraining order against me. With a shotgun with my prints all over it, I don't plan on being one of those dumb fucks who spends years in prison, trying to prove his innocence."

Sutton set her groceries on the counter, careful to make sure they were away from the blood. Then she took out her phone, but Tate jerked it from her hand.

"Who in the fuck do you think you're calling?"

"Give that back. You need an ambulance."

"Didn't you hear a word I just said? I am not going to prison. I didn't kill that piece of shit."

"You can tell the sheriff what happened—"

Tate snorted. "Do you think they're going to believe me? Everyone in town knows I hated that drunk. I'm not going anywhere until I find out who set me up."

Sutton's mouth dropped open. "You can't stay here. You're bleeding all over the place."

"Then patch me up." Tate staggered to her couch with the dish cloth pressed to his chest.

"I don't know how."

"Boil some water. You have any disinfectant?"

Sutton could see it was useless to argue with him. The stubborn man would bleed to death if she didn't help him.

Throwing him an irritated glance, she went into the bathroom, searching through the cabinets and finding hydrogen peroxide and some gauze. Carrying both back to the living room, she went to the kitchen to place a kettle of water on to boil.

"Help me get this off." Tate was trying to pull off his shirt, which was drenched in blood.

Setting down the disinfectant and gauze on the end table by the couch, she then helped Tate take off his shirt. His face was pasty white, and he was covered in a sheen of sweat when they finished.

"I'm going to throw up."

Hastily, Sutton ran to the kitchen, grabbing a bowl she had set out to pour the hot water into. Running back, she managed to place it in Tate's hands before he vomited.

She went back into the kitchen, opening one of the kitchen drawers where she found a clean dishcloth and dampened it with cold water. She went back to Tate who was still heaving into the large bowl. Placing the cloth on the back of his neck, she sat down next to him on the couch, helping him to hold the bowl.

"You have to let me call an ambulance. You're going into shock."

"No, just give me a second." He managed to lift his head, his hand dragging the cloth from the back of his neck to press it against his face.

"Finished?"

Tate nodded weakly, leaning back on the couch.

"At least let me call Greer or Dustin?"

"No," he refused. "The cops will be waiting to follow them. Call Rachel. She can fix me up, and Cash can sneak her in without being seen."

Sutton immediately took the phone Tate handed her, pressing the number Cash had given her.

"Hello?"

"Cash, this is Sutton."

"What's up?"

"I have Tate at my house. He's hurt. He needs Rachel."

"Tell him he's shit out of luck. I'm not letting my wife get involved with the mess he's in. Knox has already come here, looking for him. He should turn himself in."

"He didn't do it, Cash. He said someone is pinning it on him, and you and I both know no one in town will believe he's innocent." Sutton couldn't understand why she was coming to Tate's defense.

"Fuck!" She heard him talk to someone in the background, and then Cash's voice came back on the line. "Give me five. I'll see what I can do."

"Thanks, Cash."

The line was disconnected.

"He's pretty mad," she commented.

"What's new?" Tate grunted, shifting on the couch.

She stood up and went into her bathroom to dispose of the vomit then grabbed a pillow, taking it back to the living room where she laid it down on the arm of the couch.

"Lie down," she ordered.

He fell down more than he lay down. Then Sutton went to the linen closet, pulling out several towels before going back to Tate. She pried his hand away from the dish cloth he had pressed against his stab wound, placing a clean towel down on the gaping hole. She thought she might throw up herself.

"You should go to the hospital."

"No." Tate groaned in pain when she pressed down on the towel, trying to stop the bleeding. "I should have kept my ass inside when I heard those shots."

"Yes, you should have," Sutton agreed as she heard the sound of motors from outside. "What in the world is that?"

"From the sound, I think my brother-in-law brought a few of his friends to help."

Sutton left Tate on the couch, going to the window to look outside. Her mouth dropped open at the sight of her driveway being filled with motorcycles.

"I'm not opening the door to them."

Tate gave a strangled laugh. "How many did he bring?"

"Six."

"The fucker couldn't be inconspicuous if he tried."

Sutton jumped when she heard a knock on the door.

"Let them in."

"Hell no. You're safer in jail."

From the look of the men she had seen getting off those motorcycles, help wasn't what they were going to be giving Tate. They were more likely to finish the job of his unknown assailant.

"Let them inside. They'll know how to stop the bleeding."

Sutton reluctantly went to the door. Her hand trembling, she opened the door slowly so the group of men could file inside. She stood by the door, trying to decide if she should make a run for it while she had the opportunity. Or so she thought until she noticed one of the bikers standing outside the door with his arms crossed against his chest. He was wearing sunglasses and covered in tattoos.

Sutton slammed the door in his face, deciding she was safer inside.

Cash stood behind the couch, staring down at Tate while one of his friends went around the couch to squat down next to him, checking on his wound.

"What in the fuck happened?"

"Someone knocked me out, and then the bastard stabbed me while I was out and planted the gun on me that killed Lyle," Tate answered Cash's question, his voice filled with pain.

"You sure you didn't do it?"

"I believe I would know if I blew someone's brains out." Tate tried to shift away from the man who had picked up the disinfectant and gauze to clean his wound. "Dammit, Train, do you have to be so rough?"

"You want me to stop the bleeding?" the man answered without remorse, continuing to work on him.

Tate's mouth snapped closed.

Sutton went into the kitchen, turning off the boiling water. Using a hot pad, she carried the water into the living room, setting it on the coffee table so the biker named Train could reach it.

When he shrugged off a small backpack, pulling out several items, she moved back, watching as he cleaned Tate then methodically sutured the wound. The other bikers stood silently as Tate cussed.

"Rachel could have fixed me up without making me wish I had bled to death."

Cash's mouth tightened. "Maybe so, but I'm not putting my child at risk because you're a pussy."

"Rachel's pregnant?"

Cash nodded.

"She didn't tell me."

Sutton squashed the sympathy that his words stirred.

"She was going to tell you this weekend when we came over to dinner after Holly and Logan came home. She wanted to tell you all together."

"Oh, I'm glad you didn't tell her, then."

"I told her. I don't keep any secrets from my wife. She understood why I didn't want her to come. She wouldn't have been able to stop herself from helping you."

Train stood up, reaching into his backpack and pulling out three bottles of pills. "One is for pain, one for infection, and the last one is an iron pill. All three of them are marked."

Sutton took them from him.

"Give me one of those pain pills and some whiskey if you have it."

"I don't, but I have some beer."

"That'll have to do."

Sutton went to get his beer, offering it to him after Cash helped lift him so he could swallow the pills then laid him back down. Tate's eyes closed before his head was back on the pillow.

"What am I supposed to do?" Sutton asked Cash when the group of men went to the door.

"Keep his wound clean and dry for a few days. It shouldn't take that asshole more than a couple of days before he's back on his feet."

"I can't take care of him for that long. The police are looking for him, and I'm not going to jail for being an accessory."

Cash's lips twitched. "I'll keep Knox off your property until Tate's up and around and can figure out who attacked him. I'll go by and let Greer know he's okay. Maybe, between him and Dustin, they can figure out who wanted to pin Lyle's murder on him."

"You don't think he did it, either?"

"Fuck no. If Tate killed Lyle, he would be bragging about it, not hiding out. Keep inside the house and don't let anyone in but me and Knox."

"Why would the sheriff help?" Sutton asked, confused.

"Because he's a friend of mine. He'll give Tate a few days' head start to clear his name. After that"—Cash shrugged—"he'll have to find some other place to hide out. As long as it's not my house, I really don't give a fuck. If he hadn't pissed off most of the town, people would be more likely to believe in his innocence."

Sutton silently agreed. Tate and his brothers would never win a popularity contest. Most of the townspeople would probably cheer if he was locked up.

Sutton stood in the doorway, watching the men ride away with mixed feelings. The bikers were intimidating on *and* off their bikes.

She checked on Tate, seeing he was asleep. His cheeks were flushed and his hair damp. Sutton's hand went to his forehead, checking for a temperature. He was warm but not hot. She hoped the antibiotic she had given him would prevent him from getting an infection.

Using the hot water, she washed his hands and chest, wiping the dried blood away. Tate didn't wake. When she finished, she pulled the blanket she kept at the foot of the couch over him then carried the dirty water to the bathroom to dump it down the drain.

Going back to the living room, she straightened up the mess, feeling her own eyes droop with fatigue. She hadn't slept last night, and it was catching up with her.

She sat down at the end of the couch, placing his feet on her lap. If he moved, she would feel it and wake up. Letting her head fall to the back of the couch, she stopped fighting to stay awake, dozing off while wondering if she had lost her mind again by trying to help a man who wouldn't appreciate it, much less thank her for risking her own freedom.

Sleepily, she opened her eyes to check on him. "You haven't changed. You never could stay out of trouble."

CHAPTER TEN

Tate woke, wondering why in the fuck he was so sore. Opening his eyes in the dark room, he stared around, disoriented. Thinking he had drunk too much the night before, it was only when his gaze fell on Sutton that his memory returned.

Wincing, he tried to maneuver his body to take the pressure off his sore ribs. His hand rubbed the spot where he was sure someone had kicked him after knocking him out.

"Can I get you something?" Sutton's husky voice drew his attention back to her.

His feet were laid casually across her lap, and her drowsy gaze hardened his dick despite his body being unable to do a damn thing about it.

"Water and another pain pill," his voice croaked out the request.

Sutton raised her arm to look at her wrist watch. "It's almost time for it, anyway."

She scooted out from under his feet, stiffly rising to go the kitchen. It was only a moment before she was back, holding out the pain pill and a bottle of water.

Tate took the pill, chasing it down with the water thirstily.

"I'll heat you up some soup. If you don't eat something, the medication will make you sick." She didn't wait to hear if he wanted it or not, going back to the kitchen.

Tate tiredly rested his head back on the pillow, listening to her movements in the kitchen. When he smelled the soup, his stomach growled.

"What time is it?"

"Three in the morning," Sutton said, coming back, carrying the cup of soup and setting it on the end table. Then she helped him to rise to a sitting position, and he thought he might pass out.

"The blood you lost will make you dizzy for a while. The knock on your head will make it worse." She sat down next to him, handing him the soup.

His hand shook when he took it from her.

"Careful. It's hot," she warned.

Tate took a small sip, feeling as if he would hurl it up immediately. Sutton's hand under the cup encouraged him to take another drink.

"The more you drink, the less you'll feel sick."

"Why in the fuck do you care?" Tate regretted the harsh words as soon as they left his mouth. His throbbing dick was aggravating the hell out of him. How could he still be attracted to the cheating liar?

"I don't." Her hand dropped to her lap.

"Sorry," he mumbled. "You're being nice by letting me stay here, and I was being an ass."

Sutton gave him a cold smile. "It comes naturally to you and your brothers. That's why you're holed up here."

"We're not ass-kissers; that's for sure."

"You're in your thirties now, Tate. Don't you think it's time you grew up?"

His mouth twisted. "That's twice this week I've been told that."

Her head tilted to the side. "Who else said that to you?"

"Your father."

Her expression became even more remote. "Then that's the first thing we've agreed on in years."

"Really? According to him, you haven't talked to him in years. He said to tell you to call your mother, she's not doing well."

Sutton stood up, going to the window to look out, remaining silent.

"Must have been a pretty bad argument to cause a rift between you and your parents. From what I remember, you three were pretty tight."

"Things changed." She didn't turn around or elaborate on the distance that had developed between her and her parents.

At one time, she would have told him without asking. She had been an open book. Now, she was closed off emotionally and physically, not just from him, but others who had been important in her life. Could her husband's death have affected her so badly?

"Your father said you're a widow."

"Is that all he told you?"

"Yes. Why?"

"No reason, just curious. I didn't know if he knew Scott was dead."

"That must have been some fight you had with them."

Sutton turned back from the window. "Can I get you some more soup?"

He shook his head. "I'll be lucky if I can keep this down."

Without a word, she left the room. She was gone several minutes, and he was beginning to wonder if she had gone to bed when she returned.

"I made Pap's bed for you. You'll be more comfortable there." She held her hand out to help him up from the couch.

Tate stared at it for a second before taking it, trying not to give her too much of his weight. He grimaced as the pain in his chest and ribs nearly made him fall back, but Sutton grabbed his belt, steadying him.

"Put your arm over my shoulder," she ordered.

Tate hesitated, but he knew he couldn't make it to the bedroom alone, and if he spent another minute on the old couch, he would be a cripple come morning.

He placed his arm over her shoulder as they walked in the direction she led him.

"Do you want to use the bathroom before you lie back down?"

"Yes."

She opened the door next to the open bedroom door, leading him inside after she flicked on the light switch.

"Open the door when you finish," Sutton said, leaving the bathroom and closing the door behind her.

Tate used the toilet then went to the bathroom sink. The man reflected in the mirror wondered how Sutton didn't believe him capable of killing Lyle. His hair was plastered to his head, and he had a drugged-out look in his eyes. He looked like a serial killer.

He ran the water, making it as cold as he could. Using his hand, he splashed water onto his face and hair. When he finished, he opened the door to find Sutton waiting patiently.

He let her help him into the bedroom where he dropped onto the mattress, feeling too weak to bend over and take off his boots. As Sutton crouched down in front of him, doing it for him, Tate felt his dick stirring again.

She glanced up, catching him staring at her.

"Do you need some help to get out of your jeans?"

He was tempted to ask for her help, but decided his dick wouldn't be able to handle her hands anywhere near his belt buckle.

"I can do it."

Sutton nodded. Going to the boxes stacked against the wall, she rummaged through the one on top, pulling a pair of pajama pants and top from inside. She handed them to him.

"They might be a little short, but they should fit well enough."

"I usually sleep naked," he taunted to see what kind of reaction he would get.

"Go for it, but if the state police come to arrest your ass, don't blame me if they carry you out of here with your dick flapping."

Unable to help himself, he laughed then held his ribs from the pain it caused.

"You've become sassy. At one time, you would have turned bright red and taken off."

"I'm not seventeen anymore."

"No, you're not," he agreed, his eyes going to her full breasts and curvy hips.

She ignored his appreciative gaze. "Do you need anything else? If not, I'm going to bed."

"You ever regret dumping me for Cash?" Tate didn't know why the question came out of his mouth other than it had been one he wanted answered.

"Really?" She stared down at him angrily. "You want to ask that at three in the morning?"

"Never mind. I don't give a fuck about the answer, anyway." He wasn't about to let her think it had bugged him over the years.

"If you didn't want to know, then why ask? No, I never regretted Cash. What's wrong, Tate? Does it burn your Porter pride that you weren't the one who broke up with me?"

"You were replaced"—he snapped his fingers—"like that."

Her mouth gave a curl of contempt. "Do you honestly think I didn't know that? The Monday after prom, half a dozen of my friends told me by the end of first period that you spent the night with Lisa in the motel room you had reserved for us."

He stiffened as he sat on the side of the bed. For a split-second, the controlled mask she kept on her face had dropped, and her agony and humiliation were revealed before being concealed once again by her nonchalance.

"Sutton…"

"Forget it. It didn't matter then, and it doesn't now." She went out the door, leaving him alone, heading into the bedroom across the hall.

He wanted to go after her; instead, he changed into the pajamas she had given him then lay down on the bed after turning off the bedside lamp.

He stared up at the ceiling as the hurt she had shown played over and over in his mind. Had she regretted breaking up with him? Had it been a ploy to get him jealous?

Tate didn't even know why it mattered after all this time. Then again, the sexual chemistry was still there between them, so maybe he wanted a taste of what he had been denied back then. Maybe he wanted to even the score and be the one to dump her this time.

Tate closed his eyes, the pain pill finally making him drowsy enough to ignore the pain. He wouldn't be able to leave for the next few days. If he was lucky, he would finally be able to put his past with Sutton to rest. He wasn't a kid anymore, and neither was she. Sutton was a widow. She probably had a couple of lovers before she married, and after the death of her husband. They both were adults, and if he decided he wanted to get her out of his system, there was nothing to stop him, not even Sutton.

CHAPTER ELEVEN

Sutton stretched, yawning, feeling as if she hadn't slept at all. She looked at the clock on her bedside table.

A scream escaped her when she saw a man standing at the window outside her bedroom.

"Shut up!" Greer's loud voice could be heard through the glass.

Sutton stormed toward the window, unlocking it then raising it halfway. "What in the world are you doing outside my window?"

"I'm not a damn pervert. Let me in; I want to talk to Tate."

"Why didn't you just go to the door?" She stubbornly refused to budge.

"I didn't want the cops to see me."

"What cops?" Sutton became frightened that her pap's home was going to be raided. Visions of police raids ran through her mind.

"The ones watching me. Now move."

"Let him in," Tate ordered from behind her.

Her fingers trembled when she realized he was standing so close to her.

She raised the window the rest of the way before sliding sideways so she wouldn't touch Tate's bare chest. She was glad he had at least worn the pants, although they were loose and hung low on his hips. His muscular body was illuminated by the early-morning sun shining through the window.

Unconsciously, she licked her bottom lip, lowering her eyes when she saw Tate was staring at her. Realizing he wasn't the only one half-dressed, she snatched up the robe she had placed on her bed the night before, coving the thin T-shirt that came to the top of her thighs.

Greer climbed in through the widow with a dexterity that showed it wasn't the first time he had used the method to enter a home.

Once he was inside, he studied his older brother with a critical eye. "You okay?"

"Been better," Tate answered, his hand holding his ribs.

"What happened?"

As Tate started to describe to Greer what had happened, Sutton interrupted long enough to tell them she was making coffee.

"Close the curtains in the living room."

Sutton stopped, glaring at Greer's order. "I will. I've already been frightened once this morning. If I look out and see Dustin's face, I'll have a heart attack."

Greer ignored her jibe, turning back to question Tate.

Sutton made a pot of coffee and toast for herself. She drew the line at feeding Tate. He could fix his own breakfast.

She was about to take a bite of the grape jelly smeared toast when Tate and Greer entered the kitchen, taking chairs at the table.

"Can I get a cup of coffee?"

"I'm not a waitress. Get Greer to pour you a cup."

Both brothers stared at her mutely before Greer's chair scraped back and he went to the coffee pot, pouring them both a cup.

"Why are you holding your ribs?"

"The son of a bitch must have kicked me while I was unconscious," Tate answered with a grimace as he tried to get comfortable on the chair.

"Want me to tape you up?"

"No. I think they're just bruised. I'm not having trouble breathing, so nothing's broken."

"You're damn lucky whoever did it didn't kill you."

"They didn't want me dead. If they did, they had the chance when I was unconscious."

"Any idea who it could be?"

"No." Tate ran his hand through his hair. "Go see Jo today and see if she knows why her dad was out in the woods so late."

Greer set their cups down on the table before sitting back down.

Tate took a drink then asked for his pain pills. Sutton went into her bedroom to get the pills, and when she came back, they were discussing the different people in town who had grudges against Lyle.

"Lucky is still angry that he nearly ran Willa over when he was drunk."

"Lucky wouldn't have killed him. He's a pastor. He would have sent Shade after him, and that bastard doesn't shoot from behind; he likes to pop them between the eyes."

"How do you know that?"

"I saw him take someone out when he didn't know I was watching."

Sutton slid her plate of toast to Tate, not wanting him to get sick on an empty stomach. Greer reached out, taking a piece of the toast. That was when she decided, if she was going to get anything to eat, she was going to have to feed them first. She made a stack of toast and nuked a couple of packets of oatmeal.

Setting the food down, she snatched one of the toast slices before the men could take it all.

She chewed on the toast as Greer filled Tate in on the different agencies searching for him.

"The state police came by during the middle of the night. They tore the house apart then went to Cash and Rachel's house."

"They tear it apart, too?"

"What do you think? Cash was standing there, watching every move they made."

"They were too afraid of Cash to tear his house apart, but you let them tear ours apart? I'm disappointed in you."

"Fuck off," Greer grumbled. "I wasn't there. I was in the woods with Dustin, trying to find any signs of who killed Lyle."

"Find anything?"

"No."

"If Jo doesn't know anything, ask if she will let you look through Lyle's room."

"I'll try. Probably won't be anything left once the police are done."

Tate shrugged. "They might miss something."

Greer stood. "It's gonna get busy, so be careful and stay inside. The police aren't the only ones who might be searching for you."

"Leave me your gun. Whoever knocked me out took my shotgun. I stashed the one they used to shoot Lyle in our hole. When it gets dark, get it and give it to Cash. Maybe he can figure out who it's registered to."

"Will do. The only good part of this mess is that we had already cleared the land and stashed the product."

"Do you think whoever did this could have been searching for your weed?" Sutton asked the two men.

"Could be, but they'll never find it," Greer snickered. "It's probably the best batch we've grown. They would have smoked it up before turning it in to evidence."

"I doubt that."

"Don't. It's some of the best. Most of what's been grown lately is shit. The growers are trying to develop strong product for better buzz. Instead, they're making it weaker. Others are selling that synthetic shit that'll make you crazy as fuck. Ours is the best out there right now. I don't care what state you live in. Tate is the best grower around," Greer bragged.

Sutton was curious despite herself. "If Tate is the grower, what do you do?"

"I protect the fields then sell it when it's done. Anyone who comes near our fields is either going to be left a cripple or dead." He gave her a sinister grin, which ran chills down her back. She didn't doubt his words.

"What's Dustin's job?"

Greer's eyes narrowed on her. "You a Fed?" he asked suspiciously.

"If I were, would I let Tate hide out at my house?"

"You tell me."

Sutton rolled her eyes at Greer. He was still as obnoxious as he had been when he was younger.

"Dustin dries it out. Greer and I help out, but Dustin has the touch. He can tell the second it's done. The other growers dry it out too much so it has no taste and burns quicker. They sell more that way. We don't. Ours is high-quality and will give you a buzz that brings you back for more. That's why everyone wants to bring us down."

Sutton reached for the last piece of toast, smearing jelly on top. "I can't believe you're actually proud of your skills."

"Why not? Pot is legal in several states now. Hell, they're even coming up with fancy flavors," Tate, as always, defended his family business.

"For medicinal purposes," Sutton countered.

Greer snorted. "If they smoke ours, they'll damn sure feel better. I know I do."

"With all three of you smoking it, I'm surprised you have anything left to sell."

"We don't smoke it."

Sutton stared at Tate doubtfully.

"We don't. That wouldn't be good business. Greer smokes one occasionally to test the product, but other than that, we don't touch it."

"Why not?"

"It wouldn't be smart to smoke our profit away. Besides, imagine living in a candy store where you could have it any time you want. After a while, you get pretty sick of it."

"I ain't sick of it, just saving up for something big." Greer handed Tate the shotgun he had brought with him.

"What?" Sutton asked.

"I want a new truck, and it's hard to get credit in our line of work."

"You'll have enough after this season," Tate promised.

"That's what you said last year, until Logan broke his arm when he fell off the swing. The medical bills took a chunk of our cash."

"Family comes first."

"Yes, it does. I ain't complaining, just explaining." Greer slapped his brother on the back. "Take care."

"I will," Tate said, clutching his ribs. "Go by and see Diamond, tell her what happened. I'm going to need her help if I'm going to get out of this mess."

"I'll go talk to her now. She's probably already waiting for me to stop by."

Sutton remained at the table as the two brothers went back into her bedroom to let Greer slip out her window. How in the hell had she ended up letting a man suspected of murder hide out in her house? Her best course of action would be to call the state police and turn him over.

Her hand inched toward the cell phone lying on the table. Before she could grab it, though, Tate's hand reached from behind her, picking it up.

"You're not thinking of turning me in, are you?"

"You're not going to solve anything by hiding. Turn yourself in. If the sheriff is friends with Cash, he'll help you find out who killed Lyle."

"Knox is a friend of Cash's, not mine. I'm not sitting in a jail cell, hoping someone will believe me while the real killer gets away."

"Suit yourself. You were always too stubborn to listen to any advice I gave you. I don't know why I expected it to be any different now." She stood, intending to go get dressed.

"You don't have to be so pissy about it."

"I'm an accessory if I don't turn you in to the police."

"You sure you're not a Fed?"

"I don't know which Porter brother makes me want to pull my hair out more—you or Greer."

"You don't have to be so sensitive. It's a legitimate question."

"Not for a normal person," Sutton snapped back.

Stepping around him, she stomped to her bedroom to get changed. She had forgotten how aggravating the brothers could be when they were together. Alone, they were a pain in the ass. More than one made you want to shoot them.

She showered then put on her denim shorts and a plaid shirt that belonged to her pap. She had cut off the sleeves and tied the ends into a knot under her breasts. She had devised the top when she realized she hadn't packed enough summer clothes.

She left her hair damp. It would dry in the muggy heat. She needed to get an air conditioner installed if she had any hope of selling the old house. Although, it usually stayed cool during the morning or evening, the large trees giving the majority of the house a cooling shade.

She went into the living room, opening the windows to let in the slight breeze blowing outside.

Tate had settled on the couch and was flipping through the channels on the television. "This house is hotter than Hell."

Sutton went to the refrigerator, taking out a couple of beers. Handing him one, she opened hers.

"Little early to be drinking, isn't it?" His sarcastic words didn't keep him from opening his own bottle and taking a drink.

"Not when there isn't an air conditioner." Sutton rolled the ice-cold bottle against her forehead then her throat, enjoying the sensation against her skin.

Sutton noticed Tate had quit changing the channels. "Can't find anything you want to watch?"

"I wouldn't say that."

The sensual look he wore startled her with the effect it had on her. Her breasts tightened, her nipples hardening inside the thin bra she had put on. She was glad the shirt was loose enough on her that Tate wouldn't notice. She felt herself dampen against the seam of her shorts, and that shook her the most.

She had believed her sexual drive was dead. Other than appreciating the way men looked, she hadn't felt driven to have sex in so long she didn't actually remember her last time. She knew it was with her husband, but other than that, she came up blank.

Sutton had begun to believe her husband was right when he had been unable to stir her passion and said something was wrong with her. However, the stirring between her thighs now was proving him wrong. Evidently, all it took was a look from Tate, and her body could become primed.

Only two things held her back from exploring the newness of her body's reaction: Tate's hatred and her brain telling her it would be a catastrophe. If she had sex with him and it was as lackluster as it had been with Scott, then her hard won confidence would be left in shreds.

Scott had blamed her for the problems in their relationship. If she slept with someone else and it was as passionless as it had been with her husband, then she would know all the insults and criticisms he had thrown at her were her fault.

"You want to watch anything?" The suggestive tone he was using had her backing away.

"No, thanks. I need to make some calls and cancel some appointments, unless you want several workmen showing up to begin work on the kitchen."

"You sure?"

Her lips tightened. "What's the matter, Tate? Are you willing to put aside the hard feelings you have against me to get your dick sucked?"

His eyelids lowered to half-mast. "Why? Is sucking my dick on your mind? You sucking my dick wasn't a thought in my head."

"Oh…" Sutton turned bright red, angry her own words had betrayed the direction of her thoughts. "Can I have the phone, please?"

He placed the phone in her hand with a warning glint before he resumed channel-searching.

She was going to sit at the table when his next words stopped her cold.

"I wasn't thinking of you sucking my dick. I was too busy thinking about fucking you on the couch."

Sutton changed direction, escaping outside.

Her breathing was erratic at his admission. The son of a bitch had sent her running like a scared virgin. She was tempted to call the police and watch in enjoyment when they put him in handcuffs and took his ass to jail. Instead, she made the necessary calls to delay the workers indefinitely, using the excuse that she wanted a realtor to look at it before she made any improvements. Then she called Drake, telling him she was still debating about selling the property, but she would call him back when she made a decision.

The hand with the phone dropped to her side when she was done. She had a terrible feeling she was going to be sorry she hadn't handed Tate over to the police. She didn't care what the townspeople or her family would say if it came out she had been harboring a fugitive. She was more concerned that old feelings for him would be dredged up, even if she wasn't as innocent and easily susceptible as she had been.

She scolded herself while the voice in the back of her mind was telling her to run. Tate was even more attractive as a man, and that sexual awareness tugged at her body like a moth to a flame. If she didn't find a way to get him out of her house, she would be burned or consumed by the very flames that had attracted her.

Sutton placed her hand on the porch rail, the sun glinting off her wedding band. The reminder of her marriage stiffened her failing resolve.

No man, especially not Tate, was going to get close to her again, not even to scratch an itch she hadn't known could exist. She would give him a few days, and if his problems weren't resolved by then, she would call the police and have him escorted from her life once and for all.

CHAPTER TWELVE

"Where are you going?" Tate asked grumpily, setting down his beer on the end table.

Sutton paused before picking up her purse and car keys. "I'm having drinks with Cheryl. I told you this afternoon at lunch."

"What about me?"

"You'll be fine. I'm only going to be gone for a few hours."

"Take your phone in case I need to get in touch with you."

She raised the cell phone in her hand, waving it in the air before placing it in her purse. "You do that, and I'll make sure I come running," she said with an eye roll.

Tate narrowed his eyes at her. "Make sure you do."

Sutton blew out an exasperated breath. "I need to leave before I bash that beer bottle over your arrogant head."

"Why don't you give it a try and see what happens?"

She tensed, noting the escalating sexual tension. The two of them being trapped in close confines was wearing heavily on both of their nerves.

"I'll pass. I don't believe in attacking someone weaker than me." Sutton fled, sensing, like a bear with a sore tooth, she had prodded Tate one too many times.

She was parking her car in the parking lot of King's when her breathing finally slowed. Angering a Porter never turned out well. She needed to remind herself that she needed to keep a distance between them. She wasn't about to give Tate the opportunity to get physically or emotionally close to her again.

Cheryl was waiting for her at a small table. Sutton was amazed at the level of sophistication of the restaurant and bar: sleek, black, modern furniture and tables that made you want to relax and spend time there, which Sutton was sure was the effect the owners wanted.

"What do you want to drink?"

"I'll take a Malibu."

"That sounds good. I'll take one, too," Cheryl told the passing cocktail waitress.

"You're early," Sutton said, sitting down across from her.

"The store wasn't busy, so Jared let me leave early."

Sutton leaned back as the waitress set their drinks down in front of them. "It isn't difficult working with your ex-husband?"

"At first it was, but it was harder being broke all the time."

Sutton took a sip of her drink, enjoying the atmosphere of the bar. "I like this place."

"I do, too. Jared brought me here the other night for dinner."

Sutton couldn't resist giving her friend a warning. "Be careful. I know you probably still care for him. It's easy to let yourself fall back into a relationship with an ex."

Cheryl gave a bitter laugh. "Maybe I was a naïve idiot at one time, but not anymore. I know what else is out there now. I won't get taken in by Jared twice."

"I'm sorry. I know how much you loved him."

Cheryl lowered her voice, leaning across the tale so they couldn't be overheard. "The thing is I've discovered a different side to myself. In bed, Jared was all about what he wanted. He didn't care if I enjoyed it or not. I actually think he enjoyed it more if I didn't."

"I can see that." Sutton nodded. "He was very controlling of you, even in high school."

"Those days are over. I've found out that sex is better than potato chips. The more you have, the more you want."

Sutton tried not to blush at her frank talk. She had never been the type to want to discuss intimate details with her friends.

"If they're single, I've fucked them."

Sutton couldn't bite back the question on her lips. "Any of the Porter brothers?"

Cheryl lost her eagerness to share. Leaning back, she picked up her drink, and Sutton had the answer she didn't want.

"Which one, or more than one of them?"

"Sutton..."

She shrugged. "It's not a big deal. Tate and I were over before I graduated."

"The brothers don't fuck the same woman. I would go to Mick's after The Last Riders were finished with me, and the Porters showed me a good time, bought me drinks, and danced with me. We had a lot of fun."

Sutton had heard enough. She started to change the subject, but Cheryl had lost her reticence and gave more information than she wanted.

"Greer is too intense for me, and Dustin was too young..." Her voice trailed off. "I wouldn't have touched Tate if I thought you still cared about him. It was only a couple of times. He made it plain it was just sex, he wasn't going to get serious with me."

"That was more than he did for me." Sutton lifted her glass, draining it, then motioned for the waitress to bring her another.

"You and Tate?"

"No, we never had sex, only fooled around a little bit when we were dating."

Cheryl blew out a relieved breath. "That's good. I would hate to think it would cause a problem between you and him."

"Why would it cause a problem? I don't care whom he's slept with in town."

"He doesn't do much sleeping," she wisecracked, and Sutton wanted to throw her drink in the woman's face. "I wonder which woman he's holed up with while he's hiding out from the cops. I wouldn't mind if he wanted to hide at my place. I wonder if he's still answering his phone."

Sutton paid the waitress for the second round of drinks. Before she left, she ordered a screwdriver.

"I haven't finished my first drink."

Sutton lifted her glass toward her, giving an imaginary toast. "Then you need to catch up."

Cheryl took a long drink. "I never turn down a free drink."

"I bet you don't turn many things down." Sutton bit her lip, angry at herself. Why should she be angry at her for having sex with Tate?

"Turned down Jared," Cheryl snickered. "Does it make me a bad person that I get a kick out of him knowing I'm fucking anything with a dick, and he can't do a damn thing about it?"

"Cheryl, you shouldn't be doing it if the only reason you are is to make Jared angry."

"Did I tell you that Jared had a vasectomy, and he didn't tell me? He didn't want me or his mistresses to get pregnant. I tried for five years to get pregnant and was about to take fertility treatments, and he didn't once open his fucking mouth."

Sutton could see the anger and hurt Cheryl was trying to get out of her system. If sleeping with the men Jared had to come in contact with helped, then Sutton wasn't about to throw any stones.

"Then, no, it doesn't make you a bad person." There was no pain worse than being cheated on by the one you love.

"I'm thinking of leaving Treepoint when I get enough money saved up."

In Treepoint, it didn't matter how many women men slept with, but a woman with multiple sexual partners was labeled with only one title—slut.

"It might help take away some of the resentment you're feeling toward Jared."

"You don't by any chance need a roommate, do you?"

"I'm afraid I already have a roommate, and I don't think you and Stella would hit it off. I have a couple of friends who are looking for another roommate, though. If you're interested, I could give you their numbers."

"I would appreciate it. If I find a roommate, then I could move sooner."

Sutton took out her cell phone, sending her the two phone numbers. "I think you would have a lot in common with Kazzie and Soria."

"I'll call them tomorrow. Thanks, Sutton."

"Don't thank me until you talk to them. Are you sure you want to do this? All your family is here."

"They haven't had anything to do with me since The Last Riders, so I'm really not too concerned with what they have to say."

Sutton shook her head. "It's not going to be as easy to leave as you think. The mountains are hard to leave. They stay in your blood."

"If you missed it so badly, why did you stay away so long?"

"I didn't have anything to come back for."

* * *

Sutton let herself into the dark house, locking the door behind her. She crossed the floor, bumping into the couch. Unable to help herself, she started giggling.

"I see you had a good time." Tate's voice came from the chair beside the couch.

"I did." She grabbed on to the back of the couch to steady herself.

"You drove yourself home in this condition?"

"No, one of Cheryl's friends gave us a ride."

"Cheryl doesn't have any friends. Who was it?"

"She does, too. I'm one, and some guy named Rider."

"How did Rider drive you and Cheryl home? He rides a bike, and both you and Cheryl wouldn't fit on it at the same time."

"Train gave her a ride."

"I bet that won't be the only ride he gives her tonight." Tate's sarcastic tone raised her simmering anger.

"Jealous it's not you?" she said snidely. "Give her a call. She would be more than willing to give you a place to hide out."

"You told her I was here?" She saw his shadow rise from the chair angrily.

"No. She was just talking about you and mentioned she wouldn't mind you hanging out at her place."

"Why was she talking about me?"

"She was comparing you to her other lovers," Sutton lied. "She said you sucked. It's good to know I didn't miss out on anything."

"You bitch. You're lying."

"Am I?" she taunted, drunk enough that she didn't care how angry she made him. "Maybe I am; maybe I'm not. Why don't you ask her when you go stay with her? I'll even drive you myself when I sober up."

Tate's shadow moved closer to her. "What's the matter? You're the one sounding jealous. Did it make you mad that I fucked your best friend?"

Sutton held the couch as she took off her heels one at a time, dropping them to the floor. "You're too fucking funny. Cheryl isn't the first friend of mine you fucked. You nailed most of my friends even before the summer we were together. It's why I didn't sleep with you. I didn't want to be just another notch on that shotgun."

"How do you know—"

"That the row of scratches on the barrel of your rifle is how many women you've had? Greer told me. He thought it was funny. Every time we went anywhere and came back, I saw him looking at your rifle, so one day, I asked him."

"Why would he tell you?"

"Because I offered him a twenty if he told me. Greer may be your brother, but cold cash is king with Greer."

"I'm going to kick his ass."

"Why? It was a long time ago, and it's not like it made a difference with me. I was stupid enough to believe anything you told me, hook, line, and sinker." She gave a self-deprecating laugh. "What are you waiting for, Tate? Don't you want to rub my face in how many of my friends you fucked, how you paid me back for betraying you?"

"I only fucked one woman because I wanted payback. The others were because I was horny."

"You make me sick," she snarled at him, shaking in anger.

"Yeah? I don't believe that for a second. I think you're mad because you were too scared to fuck me then, and you're too scared to now. You want to know the difference between Lisa, Cheryl, and you? They weren't afraid to take what they want."

"I don't want you, you arrogant ass!"

"Prove it then." Tate reached out, jerking her to him, her breasts plastered against his chest.

Her hands went to his shoulders to push him away, not wanting to hurt him by shoving them against his chest. When her mouth came open to blast him, he caught it with his, thrusting his tongue inside.

Furious, she bit down, tasting the metal tinge of blood in her mouth. She underestimated him, though; he didn't break away. Instead, his hand went to her jaw, pressing hard so she couldn't snap her teeth closed again.

It wasn't like any of the kisses he had given her when they were younger. Then, he had been gentle with her, holding back until she would begin to respond. Now, Tate took, demanding her response by seductively exploring her mouth with experience, seeking the warm recesses as his hand cupped her bottom, pulling her closer to his hips. She felt the hardness of his cock behind the pajama pants he wore.

"Tate…" Sutton moaned.

"Don't you wonder what it would have been like between us?"

The question brought her to her senses, and regardless of whether or not she hurt him, she pushed against his chest. His hands dropped from her immediately as he took a step back.

Her hand reached out, wiping the taste of him away. "No." She started walking to her bedroom, deciding she was too drunk to deal with him.

Tate wasn't a man to push, especially since he was already climbing the walls from being confined to the house.

"You want to hear something funny?" Tate asked softly before she could escape. "When you left town, I missed you, even though I knew you had been with Cash. Did you miss me? Did you even give me a second thought?"

Sutton placed her hand on the wall, desperately trying not to sink to the floor as his words cut her like a knife to her gut.

"You didn't miss me." She leaned against the wall, turning back to face him, glad the darkness in the room hid the tears coursing down her cheeks. "I came back to town three weeks after I left, just after your case had been dismissed. I was waiting outside in my car when Lisa came out with you, holding your hand exactly how I did at your parents' funeral.

"Funny, isn't it, how you always manage to have a woman to give you support, but you sure as fuck never manage to return the favor, do you, Tate? To miss something, it has to belong to you, become a part of you. I never missed you, because you can't miss what you never had."

CHAPTER THIRTEEN

Tate heard the pain in her voice that the darkness kept hidden from him. He reached down, turning on the lamp sitting on the table at the end of the couch. Sutton blinked at him several times when the dim light flooded the room.

"I'm going to bed."

"Why did you come back?"

Her head fell back against the wall. "I don't even know. Perhaps to tell you the truth, to make you feel as miserable as I was. I honestly don't know." She brushed the tears away from her cheeks with her shaking hand. "I told myself that I only wanted to see you and explain. I couldn't bear it that you hated me, that Rachel hated me."

Tate stared at her hard, feeling as if he had overlooked something important. "What did you want to explain?"

"Nothing that matters anymore." This time, she managed to slide along the wall until she reached her bedroom. When she went inside and would have shut the bedroom door behind her, he reached his hand out, pushing the door open, and she stumbled, almost falling. Tate grabbed her arm then helped her sit down on the side of the bed.

He crouched down in front of her. "Tell me now. Pretend Lisa wasn't there that day. What were you going to tell me?"

Her lips remained stubbornly closed. Her injured pride of seeing another woman with him would never allow her to tell him.

He hadn't asked Lisa to be there that day. He hadn't been aware she was in the courtroom until the hearing was over and she had come up to him.

His hands went to each side of Sutton's hips, spreading out flat on the bed and pinning her in place.

"Go away, Tate. Just go away! God knows it won't change a damn thing."

"One thing you never learned about me is I'm stubborn as shit. I'm not going to leave until you tell me."

Sutton's shoulders slumped. "I never cheated on you with Cash."

"You went out with him, told him I broke up with you."

"I did," she acknowledged her deception. "You're not going to leave, are you?"

"No."

She sighed dejectedly. "I didn't think so." Sutton fell back on the mattress, her arm covering her eyes. She remained silent so long he thought she might have fallen asleep.

Her voice when she began talking was so matter-of-fact it was like she was discussing someone else, not them. It was as if she was distancing herself to get through the explanation so he would leave her in peace.

"My dad told me after you were arrested that he would make sure you went to jail and lose custody of your brothers and sister if I didn't break up with you."

Tate remembered the day he had called her and her father had answered the phone. He moved to sit down on the bed next to Sutton as she continued to tell him what had happened.

"I didn't know what to do. I didn't want you losing your temper with my father if you knew he was trying to break us up, so I called Cash and asked him out. I knew, when you found out, it would be over between us."

"You fucked him to keep me from going to jail?" The harshness in his voice made him wince. He felt like the ass she was calling him all the time.

He saw tears sliding down from under the arm she had pressed to her eyes.

"I didn't sleep with him. I know it seemed like I did, but I didn't. I looked like hell because my dad and I got in a fight when Cash showed up to pick me up the night before, and I fell down the steps. Cash caught me and took me to the emergency room. I spent the night there. When I got out, Cash drove me to school because I didn't want to go home."

Tate remembered how stiffly she had moved, thinking it had been because she had spent the night losing her virginity to Cash. Instead, she had been injured while trying to protect him and his family.

He bent over, burying his face in his hands. "Jesus, all you had to do was tell me, Sutton. I would have fixed it."

She gave a bitter laugh. "How exactly would you have fixed it? You would have just ended up in more trouble, so I let you believe it and went to prom with Cash. I even watched you drive away from the prom after only being there for an hour with Lisa. I left town as soon as I had that diploma in my hand."

"You came back, though."

"I knew my father would keep the agreement and drop the charges. I was hoping we could be together again, that you would see you would lose your family if you didn't quit growing weed. Then Lisa came out with you and kissed you. You want to have a good laugh? You still want payback? I'm going to give it to you. I still was going to talk to you and tell you the truth. I was getting out of the car when you went into the diner. I was going to talk to you then, but Lisa had waited for me outside the door, and she stopped me."

"She must have seen you. She told me to go on inside, that she needed to make a call. What did she say to stop you?"

"That I should leave, that you two were together, that you were going to get married."

"And you believed her? You had only been gone a couple of months. You should have known I wouldn't have married her so quickly after breaking up with you."

"I thought so, too, until she told me she was pregnant. I knew you would marry her if she was pregnant. She begged me not to interfere, saying the baby needed a father."

"I'm going to kill that fucking bitch. If she was pregnant, it wasn't my kid. I used a rubber every time I fucked her," Tate said hoarsely. He had only been with Lisa prom night and the night after she had shown up at the courtroom.

"I stayed in the same hotel you stayed with her that night. Treepoint only had the one hotel, and I was never any good with driving at night. As soon as the sun came out, I left, and you were still inside with her."

"That was the last night I spent with her. I told her the next morning that I didn't want to see her again. She was talking about moving in with me and the others."

"Are you sure she wasn't pregnant?" Sutton asked, dropping her gaze to her own abdomen.

"If she was pregnant, it wasn't mine," he stated again with certainty. He sure as fuck was going to have a talk with the lying whore as soon as he could step out in daylight again.

"Will you leave now? I'm tired."

"I'll leave, but we aren't done talking. We have a few things that need to be settled."

"We have nothing left to talk about. It won't change anything and will only dredge up memories that are better left buried."

"Secrets have a way of being dug up when we least expect them to be. I don't fucking appreciate the way you didn't have any faith in me. You didn't even give me a chance."

"I gave you a chance; you just didn't want it. You let me walk away from you. You didn't even fight for me. You nearly beat Mike Rodes to death for stealing your coon dog. I didn't mean as much to you as a damn dog."

"The dog was mine. I don't give up anything that's mine. I hadn't made you mine yet. That was my biggest mistake. I knew you were innocent, and I didn't want to push you. I shouldn't have cared that you were a virgin and just been the asshole everyone thinks I am. I won't make that mistake ever again."

Sutton's eyes widened as she lifted herself into a sitting position. "What does that mean?"

"I'm not a nice guy. Everyone in town will tell you I'm a mean son of a bitch. I should have claimed you when you were seventeen. I fucked up. I won't do that again. I'm giving you fair warning, Sutton: you're mine."

"You can't just claim me," she sputtered angrily.

"Watch me." He stared down at her confidently, his eyes settling on her breasts, seeing the erratic pulse beating at the base of her throat.

"You come near me, and I'll shoot you."

Tate walked to the door. "You can try."

"I will," she threatened.

"You're mine. You can believe that," he stressed before turning on his heel to face her again. "You want me to prove it to you now? The only reason I'm leaving is because I don't want our first time together to be when you're drunk, but if you're sober..."

She hastily shook her head. "I'm drunk."

He stared at her doubtfully. "You don't seem drunk anymore."

"I am!"

His lips quirked in a smile. She was the only one besides his family who could actually make him laugh.

"I'll see you in the morning, then. Night, Sutton."

"Go to Hell!"

"If I go, you're going with me. I'm not letting you go. My daddy would roll over in his grave if I let you get away from me twice."

"Your daddy was crazy."

"Yes, he was, and he taught me everything he knew about growing pot and women."

"I wish your mother could hear you. She would beat you over the head with her cast-iron skillet."

Tate gave her a predatory look. "I wish she was alive, too. She would tell you something, too."

"What?" she snapped.

"That you don't stand a chance."

CHAPTER FOURTEEN

A loud knocking at the front door woke her from the alcohol-induced sleep she had fallen into after Tate had finally left her bedroom last night. Hastily pulling on her robe, she opened her bedroom door and was startled when she saw Tate standing in his bedroom doorway. He placed a finger against his lips, silently telling her to be quiet.

"I have to see who it is," Sutton whispered.

Once he nodded, she padded barefoot to the window beside the door, peeking out. She saw a large figure that she didn't need to see his uniform to recognize. She turned back to Tate who was staring at her from the hallway.

"*Knox*," she silently mouthed.

At his nod, she opened the door, motioning the sheriff in before closing it behind him.

"Morning," she greeted him, though his attention was on Tate as he came farther in the room.

"Did you leave the house last night?" he asked Tate without returning her greeting.

"No."

The sheriff turned his attention to her. "Were you here with him all night?"

"No. I went out for drinks with Cheryl. Why?"

"Helen Stevens was shot and killed last night. She was found in her car that was parked in the carport. One of her neighbors heard a shot then found her. It was around eight-thirty. Were you here at that time?"

"No, I was still at King's. I didn't get home until after twelve. Why do you think Tate could have done it?"

"The state police think Tate was trying to rob her or take her car. They think he accidently shot her when she put up a fight."

"That's bullshit, and you know it," Tate snarled. "I'm not an amateur. If I shoot someone, it damn sure wouldn't be an accident."

"Are you saying you deliberately shot her?"

"Don't be fucking stupid. I didn't leave the house last night, and I wouldn't attack a woman and kill her for her car. If I wanted to get out of town, Greer or Dustin would help me. Hell, even Cash would."

The sheriff ran his hand over his bald head. "I'm going to take you in. Someone is running around town, killing people to make it look like you're responsible."

"If you take me in and the shootings stop, it's going to make me look even guiltier. The shootings *will* stop, and they'll get away while I'm locked up. That shit isn't going to happen."

"Tate, if you were in jail, that woman may still be alive." Sutton bit her lip. Was she indirectly responsible for someone's death because she had given him a place to hide?

"Maybe. Maybe not. We don't know for sure. The two shootings could be connected, or I could just have been in the wrong place at the wrong time, and he didn't want to take the time to finish me off. Increase your deputies' shifts and tell everyone in town to be careful," Tate advised.

Knox nodded. "I think whoever is doing it has their own agenda, too. But if one more person gets hurt, I'm taking your ass in, and when I come to get you, I won't be knocking on the fucking door." He pointed a finger at her. "You don't leave him alone at the house again."

"I won't," she promised.

"I'll try to find out if Lyle and Helen had anything in common. Hopefully, I can turn up something."

"Thanks," Tate said. Sutton could tell it was laced with reluctance.

Knox gave him a sharp nod.

After he left, she brushed past Tate, going to her bedroom.

"What bug crawled up your ass? I'm the one in trouble." Tate leaned against the bedroom doorway, crossing his arms over his chest.

"If I didn't give you a place to hide out, that woman may still be alive."

"I doubt it. Whoever shot her must have known what time she was supposed to come home. They were waiting for her."

"You think she knew her murderer?"

"Yes."

Fear that someone was randomly killing the townspeople had Sutton thinking of packing up and returning to California.

"So, you think it was just a coincidence that I was in town when the shooting happened? Or do you think they could have seen me and decided to use the opportunity?"

"They would have to know I'm hiding out here. Do you remember who you saw at King's? Did anyone leave after you got there?"

Sutton thought back to last night carefully. "No, I really didn't pay any attention to who was there. Do you want me to call Cheryl and ask her?"

"No, she might get suspicious. Wait until she calls you. She loves to gossip. She'll think you don't know and will call. Then you can feel out if she noticed anything strange."

"Okay."

"Why do you still wear your wedding band?"

She stared at him stupidly at the sudden change in conversation. "None of your business."

"Are you still in love with him?"

"God, no." Sutton shuddered in disgust at the thought.

"Then why wear his ring?"

"To remind me of him."

"That doesn't make any sense to me."

"It doesn't have to. It does to me, and that's all that matters."

"Did you wake up on the bitchy side of the bed?"

"Yes. That happens when the cops wake me up, wanting to know if the fugitive I'm harboring killed someone else."

"You know I didn't kill Lyle or Helen Stevens."

"Then go in and prove it the way any normal person would!" Sutton turned, scattering the neatly folded clothes out of her suitcase, searching for something cool to wear.

"Are you saying I'm not normal?"

"I don't think 'normal' fits any of the Porter brothers," she snapped.

The suitcase that was lying on two chairs pushed together fell to the floor, but she didn't try to pick it back up. She grabbed a pair of crop pants and a T-shirt. Choosing her underwear, she then turned and nearly bumped into Tate.

"Why don't you unpack your clothes?"

"Because I don't know how long I'm staying. Now, if you'll excuse me, I'm going to take a shower."

"You wear your wedding ring to remember a bad marriage and don't unpack even though you've been here a couple of weeks, and you think *I'm* the one who's not normal?"

Sutton refused to engage in any further conversation with Tate. His sharp tongue always managed a snide comeback, and the more she tried to fight back, the more she unwittingly revealed. If he was determined to have the last word, he could have it.

She closed the bathroom door then took a leisurely shower, letting the water ease the stress of the sheriff's visit and being closed in with Tate. If she didn't get rid of him, there was going to be more than one killer loose in town.

Stepping out of the shower, she dried off then wound the towel around her body as she went to the sink to brush her teeth. She was rinsing the toothpaste out of her mouth when she gave a startled scream, seeing a man's reflection in the mirror. The bathroom door burst open, and Tate came running in, carrying a rifle.

"What?"

Sutton only managed to point to the window where she now recognized Dustin. She spat out the remains of the toothpaste before furiously stomping to the window to raise it for the younger brother to climb in. When he was halfway in, Sutton lost it and began beating him on the back.

"Stop." Tate put his hand around her waist, moving her away from the window so Dustin could climb in without further attack. "At least give him a chance to defend himself."

Sutton jerked away from Tate's touch. "I'm getting sick of being scared to death by someone coming by to see you. The next one who scares me, I'm going to shoot first and ask questions later." She jerked the gun away from him before he could react then reached for her clothes.

Juggling the items, she stormed from the bathroom, going into her bedroom and slamming the door shut with her foot. Barely dried off, she tugged on the crop pants and top then dragged a brush through her wet hair and put it up in a ponytail. Then she sat down on the side of the bed and stared at the shotgun she had ripped out of Tate's hands, and her blood ran cold.

It was his rifle, the one he had said the killer had taken from him. The distinctive scratches on the barrel showing how many women he had lain with were visible. The scratches all seemed old. Either Tate had grown out of the arrogant habit, or he hadn't had sex in a long time. Sutton didn't have to wonder which it was; Cheryl had confessed they had slept together as recently as a couple of weeks ago. She guessed women he fucked more than once didn't deserve a new notch.

The sound of the brothers going into the kitchen had her curious enough to open the door and follow after them.

"Jo told Greer she had no idea why he was out in the woods. Since he wrecked his truck, he caught rides with anyone he could when he wanted to go out. She didn't know who he had caught a ride with the night of his murder. He called her three hours before he was killed to tell her he was headed to Rosie's."

The bar was just a mile up the road from her house.

"Maybe no one gave him a ride home, and he started walking to town," Sutton surmised.

"Jo said she got a call from him an hour before he was killed, but she was towing a truck, so she missed his call."

"He was walking home, and he came up on the killer, or the killer used the opportunity to kill him," Sutton thought out loud before moving to stand beside the front door, Tate's rifle held seemingly casually in her hand. Keeping both brothers in her line of sight, she lifted the butt of the rifle to her shoulder, pointing it at Tate.

"What the fuck!" Dustin took a step forward.

"Dustin, stop." Tate jerked him to a halt.

"Listen to your brother," Sutton warned.

"I'm going to take that shotgun away from you and smack that ass." Tate now took a step forward.

"Try me. You told me the killer took your gun, so how did Dustin have it?" Sutton pumped the handle, the distinctive noise bringing Tate to a sudden stop.

"I have more than one gun. I don't carry that one anymore," he explained, his brown eyes snapping in fury.

His answer explained why the notch marks seemed old and faded. She lowered the weapon.

"Do you mark the barrel of that gun when you get laid by a different woman?"

His silence had her wanting to shoot him.

"I should have known." Her eyes went to Dustin. "Do you have the same disgusting habit?"

Dustin's silence betrayed his guilt, too.

"Wow. I see you raised your brother to be a jackass, too."

"It started out as a joke—"

"Keeping track of the women you sleep with isn't funny; it's disgusting."

Sutton shoved the gun at him before she changed her mind and shot him.

"Woman, have you lost your mind? You don't handle a shotgun that way. You could have accidently shot one of us."

"My pap taught me how to handle a gun."

When both men's eyes narrowed at her, she gave them a sinister smile.

Dustin returned it with a friendly grin. "I forgot how much I like you. You fucked up when you let her get away." His eyes traveled down her body. "How do you feel about being with a younger man?"

Sutton made gagging noises.

Dustin's grin slipped. "That wasn't nice."

"The only thing worse, in my opinion, than being with a younger man would be to be with a Porter."

"What's wrong with being with a Porter? You're the one who lied and cheated on Tate. If you didn't look so good naked before you wrapped up in that towel earlier, I wouldn't even be interested."

Sutton held her hand out to Tate. "Give me the gun."

Tate took a step back, the gun held tightly in his hand. "Calm down. He's joking."

"No, I—"

"Shut up, Dustin, before I save Sutton the trouble."

"I'm going." He raised his hands up in surrender. "I left the bag of clothes I brought for you outside. Come to the bathroom, and I'll give it to you."

Tate nodded before following his brother back to the bedroom.

Sutton went into the kitchen to make herself a bowl of cereal. She was sitting at the table, eating, when Tate returned.

"You didn't make me a bowl?"

"Why don't you call one of your women to come and wait on you hand and foot?"

"A simple 'no' would have been good enough."

Sutton watched as he made himself a bowl of cereal. He was pale and moved stiffly. His overpowering presence made him seem better than he actually was. When she saw him almost drop the gallon of milk, she stood up.

"Sit down. I'll make it for you." Her fingers accidently touched his when she took the milk from him.

"Thanks." He sat down at the table as she finished making the cereal for him then set the bowl down in front of him.

"Do you need another pain pill?"

"I already took it when I was in the bathroom."

Sutton nodded as she sat back down.

"How did you meet your husband?"

She paused with the cereal-filled spoon halfway to her mouth, assessing him. His face was neutral, as if he was just trying to make conversation. Sutton ate her cereal as she decided if she wanted to answer his question.

"Come on. I'm bored being cooped up."

"So, you want me to discuss my marriage to entertain you?"

"I want you to tell me about your life because I'm interested." The sincerity in his voice broke her resolve not to discuss her disastrous marriage.

"I met Scott when I was selling pharmaceutical supplies. He was a doctor on my route."

"Was it love at first sight?"

"No, he actually asked me out several times before I agreed to go out with him. At first, I wasn't interested. He seemed to be pompous, letting the prestige of his position go to his head. One night, I gave in and went out with him." She took another bite of her cereal as she remembered back to the time when she had first started dating him.

"He seemed to loosen up while we were dating. He had a sense of humor that was wickedly funny, and I didn't feel as lonely when I was with him. He asked me to marry him on Valentine's Day. I thought it was romantic and that he loved me, so I said yes."

"You thought?"

"Looking back, I think I was more of a challenge than anything else."

"That had to hurt."

Sutton pushed her bowl of cereal away, no longer hungry. "It wasn't the first time. Seems men only want me as long as it takes them to catch me."

Tate's spoon dropped into his bowl of cereal. "That's not true."

"Yes, it is. I was the tiebreaker between you and Cash. With Scott, I was a trophy."

"A trophy?"

"I found out later that the two other doctors in his practice, who had asked me out and I refused, had a bet on who could make me change my mind."

"The fucker told you this?"

Sutton nodded. "When I told him I wanted a divorce."

"It's a good thing he's dead," he said grimly.

She stood up, going to the sink to place her dirty bowl, and then went to the front door.

"Where are you going?"

"I'm going for a walk. I'll be back in an hour."

"Sutton…"

"The conversation is over. I don't want to talk about my marriage anymore. I don't want to talk about my past with you, either. It makes me sick to my stomach that I was a fool twice in my life."

"I didn't fool you—" Tate rose to face her angrily.

"Yes, you did!" she screamed at him, losing control. "You lied to me. You told me you would always be there for me, Tate! Remember? I loved you with every breath in my body, and all you were concerned about was getting one up on Cash. I was always there when you needed me. I was there when your parents were drowned. I helped you with your brothers and Rachel. I helped you pass your college entrance exams even though you had no intention of going. I protected you from my father. Even after we broke up, I watched out for you."

Tate's face went pale. "What are you talking about?"

"When Greer was put in jail for selling drugs to an under-cover cop, I read about it in the paper. I contacted Diamond and told her I would pay her any additional fees she wanted, but I wanted Greer out of jail."

"Why didn't she tell us?"

"Because I told her not to. Even now, I'm protecting you by letting you hide out here, despite that someone else could be killed." She gave a hysterical laugh. "I never stopped being there for you, but you were never there when I needed you. Ever. Not when my parents and I fought over you, not when I was missing my family and Treepoint so badly I married a man who abused me, and you sure as hell weren't there when I needed you the most—the day my daughter died."

Chapter Fifteen

Sutton flung open the door, jumped off the porch and ran into the woods, not noticing her feet being torn up by the gravel driveway or the sticks and brambles in the woods. Running from her past, Tate, and the day she had had lost her precious eleven-month-old daughter.

She came to a stop halfway up the mountain, holding her stomach, gasping, trying to catch her breath. Sobs escaped as she threw herself down next to a tree. Holding her knees, she laid her head back on the tree as she tried to regain control.

She had been determined not to tell anyone about Valentine. When her anger at Tate had opened the floodgates, she hadn't been able to push back her words. Even as she was screaming at Tate, her mind was telling her to shut up.

"Sassy pants…"

"Don't call me that."

She sat there helplessly as Tate walked forward, squatting down in front of her. His hand reached out to cup her cheek, his large palm rough and calloused, yet the gentleness in his touch gave her the strength to stifle the cries coming from her throat.

"I thought I was doing the right thing by letting you go…"

Sutton's eyes jerked up to his; the pain he was no longer trying to hide hit her with the force of a punch to the stomach.

"I would have killed Cash over any other woman I loved, the way I loved you, but I knew you would give up your dreams up for me. I would have gotten you pregnant and kept you on the mountain. I wanted your dreams to come true, not to be sacrificed for me.

"When you left town after graduation, I almost went after you. The only thing stopping me was wanting you to have the life you deserved. I told myself that I would give you your freedom until my family was grown. Then I would drag you back to Treepoint."

"You never came for me," she hiccupped, unable to stop crying.

"I did," he said, tears brimming in his eyes. "I gave you enough time to graduate and work a few years, long enough to decide which life you would prefer. I tracked you down in San Diego and waited outside where you worked. I sat there all day, waiting for you to come out. I had bought a new outfit so I wouldn't embarrass you when you saw me.

"When you came out, you looked so beautiful I couldn't move. Then, a red sports car pulled in, and a man got out, holding the door for you. I could tell he had money. He was dressed in an expensive suit with his hair all slicked back. You kissed him before getting in the car. I saw the ring on your finger and knew you were going to marry him.

"How could I compete with him? The pants I had on didn't cost as much as those fancy shoes he wore. I couldn't give you the house or the money or life he could, so I left. I was jealous and angry, but I left because you were living the life I thought you wanted and deserved. If I had any idea you needed me, I would have been there. I swear, Sutton, I would have been there for you." He sat down next to her, placing his arm around her shoulder then pulling her to him until her head lay on his shoulder.

They sat there quietly for hours, each regretting the missed opportunities. She believed Lisa's lies, and Tate had believed he couldn't measure up. Neither of them had faith in the love they had found that one special summer.

"How did your daughter die?" Tate eventually asked.

"After Scott and I were married, it didn't take long for me to realize my mistake. We had only been back from our honeymoon for two weeks when he started abusing me.

"I was taking a bath when he walked in and asked why I hadn't quit my job after he had asked me to. I told him I had never said I would quit working, and he dragged me out of the bathtub by my hair and beat me. I lay there on the wet floor, believing I was going to die.

"When he finished, he left me to go to bed as if nothing had happened. It took me a while, but I managed to get up and clean myself up. I tried to leave, and he told me if I did, he would kill my parents. I believed him. He was crazy and wasn't trying to hide it any longer. The next day, he called my work and told my boss I wouldn't be back. I was even afraid to visit pap before he died.

"Not one person called to check on me, and I didn't know where to turn to for help. I didn't want my parents to know I had married a man who would hurt me, but could potentially hurt them. I was ashamed and angry at myself for falling for his crap.

"He made sure I was isolated and afraid. I became that woman I swore I would never be when I heard about abused women. He would beat me and then hold me and say it was for my own good. I began to believe him. He stole my self-respect; I couldn't ever make him happy. If I cooked him something, he would call it slop or hillbilly swill. I used to be a good cook, remember?"

"The best I ever had." Tate's soft voice sent a wave of reassurance, though Scott's insults still had her doubting if there was truth to his statements.

"He broke my arm when he found out I was taking birth control. Then, when I didn't get pregnant, he would call me an infertile bitch. If he didn't like the way I was dressed, he would call me a slut. I wouldn't wear anything low-cut or sleeveless, even though I stayed in the house all day. I couldn't go to the grocery store unless he went with me, and he had alarms on the windows and doors that would tell him if I tried to leave. I was trapped and didn't know how to get away.

"When I became pregnant, the beatings stopped, but he wouldn't even let me go to the obstetrician alone. He stayed with me every second, even during the exams. It still boggles my mind that, because of his position, he was given so much leeway. Even professional, educated people abuse their spouses. It isn't based on being poor."

"I know that," he assured her.

"I wish my obstetrician had known that. One of the questions when I was admitted to the hospital to have Valentine was whether I was afraid of anyone. She asked me in front of Scott. How was I supposed to answer? I was too afraid to tell the truth. God help me, I should have. My daughter would still be alive."

"Sutton, I learned a long time ago that 'what' and 'if' are the two most painful words in the world. I still blame myself for not going fishing with my parents the day they died."

"I want her back so badly. Sometimes, I can't breathe because I want it so much..." She broke off as tears she didn't know how she was still capable of crying slid down her cheeks.

Tate's arm tightened around her, giving her the strength to finish the horrific account of the way her beautiful daughter's life had ended.

"When I came home from the hospital with my baby, he became even more controlling, saying I didn't want to have sex anymore. It was true. I couldn't fake it. He made my skin crawl when he touched me.

"Scott was critical of everything. I wasn't holding her right or making her take naps. He made me write down the times I breastfed her and for how long. One day, he shoved me when I was holding Valentine, and I almost dropped her. He blamed me, of course.

"When she was three months old, she developed colic, and he said the foods I was eating were to blame, giving her gas, so he made me put her on formula." Sutton began shaking, the memories becoming too painful.

"One night, he came home from working an emergency, and he went to bed. I couldn't get Valentine to quit crying. I tried everything, but she wouldn't stop. Scott came into the nursery, and I could tell by the way he was looking at her that, if he had the chance, he would hurt her. I laid her back in the crib and told him to stay away from her. When I woke up, I was lying on the floor, and he was sitting on the rocking chair, holding my baby. He said he would kill me if I ever tried to come between he and his daughter, and that was the end of it for me. I wasn't going to take the chance he would hurt Valentine again.

"When he went to bed, I slipped into the bedroom and stole his cell phone. I called a domestic abuse hotline, and the next day when Scott went to work, two of the most beautiful women in the world showed up at the door. I took Valentine and the clothes on our back and ran.

"They gave us a place to stay where Scott couldn't find us, clothes, and food. Without their help, I don't know what I would have done. They helped and counseled me through my divorce, provided me with doctors that could testify to the damage he had done to my body. He had broken my arm, several ribs, my nose had been broken so many times it was deformed, and my left eye drooped.

"I was given a divorce and a restraining order for both me and Valentine. I didn't even ask for spousal or child support, because I knew it would infuriate him even more, so they helped me find a job and start over.

"For two blissful months, I had a life that I was beginning to enjoy. Scott stayed away. I should have known he wouldn't let us go. I had even warned my parents through one of the domestic abuse shelters to be careful. I thought Scott would be too afraid of losing the respect of his friends and co-workers to violate the restraining order.

"I went to pick up Valentine from daycare two months after our divorce. When I was buckling her into her car seat in the backseat, he knocked me out and pushed me into the car. I woke up with him driving around the city, ranting at me. I tried everything I could to calm him down, but it didn't work.

"He pulled off the road and dragged me to the trunk of the car and shoved me in, slamming the lid down before I could escape. I was so proud of myself for buying that piece of junk so I would have my independence and be able to pick up Valentine from daycare. It was so old it didn't have the emergency release for trunks." She gave a bitter laugh. "I kept screaming at him to stop and let me out, that he better not hurt Valentine.

"I don't know how long he drove around, because I was in and out of consciousness. I woke when he stopped the car and threw Valentine at me. I held her as he drove, not having any idea of what he was going to do next. I don't think he did, either. I was so scared, and all I could do was lay there in the dark, holding Valentine."

"Jesus."

"Believe me, I prayed. I prayed for God to help me. I prayed my parents would save us, though I hadn't talked to them in years. I even prayed that you would rescue me. I know it was unrealistic, but I kept praying someone would save us in time.

"Finally, the car stopped, and everything was quiet. I wanted the trunk to open, but I was afraid at the same time. I was terrified of what he would do to us when it did. I heard the sound of a gunshot, but after that, nothing. I started screaming for help over and over again, pleading for Scott to open the trunk, but he never did.

"I lay there in that trunk, thinking sooner or later, I would get help. None came. Even when I knew my baby was dying, I still held out hope someone would find us in time. No one did, and when she took her last breath, I didn't want to be saved anymore. I wanted to die with her.

"When I heard someone at the trunk, I didn't make a sound. I wanted them to go away. It's funny, but when I quit wanting to be found was when I was.

"I fought the deputy who tried to help me. It took two EMTs to get me out of that trunk and take my baby away. In the hospital, they told me Scott had parked in an isolated parking lot, gotten in the back seat, and shot himself. One of the abuse workers I had remained in contact with had reported me missing, and all the members had banded together to search for us. One of them found the car in the parking lot."

Tate had remained silent so long she raised her head, finding his own eyes brimming with tears and his cheeks wet.

"If I hadn't left that day…"

"If I hadn't listened to Lisa…"

Tate's tortured expression had her protective instincts rising. She couldn't bear to see the big, outrageously confident man believe he was responsible for any part of the disaster her life had become with Scott.

"It was no one's fault besides mine. I should have brought Valentine back to Treepoint, but my pride held me back. I didn't want to face my parents with my mistake. I didn't want to see you around town, hating me, gloating that I was divorced."

A groan passed his lips.

"I'm making it worse, aren't I?"

"That you thought I was the biggest walking asshole imaginable? You were wrong. I wouldn't have gloated. I would have been chasing after you."

"Yeah, right. You didn't exactly welcome me back to town."

"Maybe not, but I wasn't able to stay away, either. Why do you think I was out in the woods the night Lyle was killed?" He picked up one of her hands, turning it over and rubbing the scarred flesh of her wrist with his thumb. "You..."

"In the hospital, without Valentine, I didn't want to live. I think Scott didn't shoot us because he wanted us to die a slow, painful death, but the bastard didn't have the courage to do it himself. I locked myself in the bathroom and slit my wrists with a razor I stole from a male patient's room next to mine. A nurse found me in time, and they managed to save me."

"Are you still suicidal?" No one would ever accuse a Porter of being tactful.

"No, I received counseling and the support of the domestic violence group that helped rescue me." She gave him an ironic smile. "It didn't take long for my mountain blood to kick back in. I decided to live just to spite Scott. It wasn't much of a reason to keep living, but then I began helping other abused women. I put them in contact with those who could help, plastic surgeons to repair physical damage that is a constant reminder of the abuse they suffered." She ran a finger down her perfectly shaped nose. "The worst thing is to be reminded every time you look in a mirror."

"I'm thankful they were there for you." Tate lifted her hand to his mouth, his lips delicately brushing the scars on her wrist.

"I don't give Scott any power over me any longer, but my wedding band reminds me not to trust in my heart ever again. It's let me down two times."

"Your heart didn't let you down; the men you loved did," Tate said. "I can't change the past. I would give my own life to bring back your daughter for you, but I can't. I can only prove I'll be there for you from now on."

Sutton pulled away from him, tugging her hand out of his firm grip. "I'm not going to give you or any other man another chance. I'm finally content with my life."

"You might have a million reasons not to trust me when I tell you I want to start over with you."

Sutton shook her head. There was no way she would have a relationship with Tate. He might crack the wall she had created around her heart to protect it.

"Don't say 'no' yet. We'll take it slow. I'll even let you set the rules."

She stared at him doubtfully. Tate letting a woman be in control was beyond his capability.

He grinned at her expression then stood and reached down to pull her to her feet.

"You might have a million reasons not to trust me, but I only need one chance to prove you wrong." He lifted her into his arms.

"Tate, put me down! You can't carry me down this mountain. You're too weak. You'll fall!"

He buried his face in her neck and she slid her arms around his neck, careful not to press against the wound on his chest.

"Your heart is telling you to give me a chance…Look where we are, Sutton."

She gazed around her, and it took her only a moment to realize where they were. It was the exact spot where they used to meet when they were teenagers, where they would lie on the old quilt and talk about their future.

Like a wounded animal, she had unconsciously sought the place she had found her greatest happiness, feeling safe in Tate's arms.

Her heart was telling her what her mind wouldn't accept: she was going to give him another chance.

CHAPTER SIXTEEN

"You're cheating," Sutton accused him.

"No, I'm not."

"Yes, you are. You said we could move at my speed. You walking around the house half-naked is cheating."

Tate gave her a saccharine smile. "It's hot."

Sutton couldn't disagree with him. He was hot, and his body awakened desires she hadn't felt in years, reminding her she was still a flesh-and-blood woman. She unconsciously licked her bottom lip when she noticed the growing bulge in his jeans.

Tate was leaning back on the kitchen counter, drinking a beer, wearing jeans that fell to his hip bones. He wasn't wearing a shirt, which showed off his broad shoulders. The man was rock-hard. He didn't have a six-pack; he was too muscular for that.

The sexual tension was building, every time she came in contact with him, the hair on her arms would stand up from the electric charge that passed between them.

"Want a sip?"

"No, thanks."

"I thought, from the way you were staring, you wanted some."

Sutton gritted her teeth. The man was too experienced not to know that she was attracted, just like a cat wanting catnip.

"If I want one, I'll get one all by myself," she taunted.

"Really? Can I watch?"

"Sure." Sutton walked to the fridge, taking out a beer and popping the top. Taking a drink, her eyes met Tate's. The tension between them escalated with the deliberate challenge in her gaze.

Tate slammed his beer down on the counter then made a sudden move toward her.

Her desire died as she took a step back.

Tate stopped a few feet away from her, his chest heaving as his hands clenched at his sides.

"Sassy pants, I can take the teasing, but I can't take the fear. I would never hurt you. I would give you my rifle to shoot me if I ever did."

Her body relaxed against the counter. "I believe you."

"You better." He slowly walked closer, placing a hand on each side of her on the counter, pinning her in place. "I'm not going to rush you. You deserve to be courted and made to feel special."

"You're not exactly a man I would take for being patient."

Tate gave her a seductive look. "I'm very patient."

A nervous laugh escaped her as she placed her hands on his shoulders, pushing him back. "I need to cook dinner. Go into the living room and finish your beer."

Tate was turning to head that way when a knock sounded on the kitchen window at her back.

"Are your brothers ever going to come to the front door?" She stared at Greer who was gawking at her from the other side of the glass.

"I think he and Dustin are getting a kick with all the sneaking around. Don't spoil their fun."

"I'd rather kick them in the ass." Sutton pushed the window up higher so Greer could clamor inside. "Don't knock anything over," she sneered at him.

She quickly moved the crockpot of beans she had spent the day cooking, if the big goof knocked them over, she would knock him over the head with the pan of fried potatoes sitting on the stove.

"Do I smell soup beans?" Greer sniffed the air, his feet still hanging from the window. "And cornbread?"

"No," Sutton lied. Deliberately, she reached out, tugging his feet loose.

"Wait…" Greer fell to the floor and glared up at her.

"Sorry."

"I bet." Greer stood, picking up his baseball cap from the floor and placing it back on his head. "Woman, you have a vicious streak, but I can deal with it if you give me a bowl of those beans."

Sutton raised a brow, remaining still.

Greer sighed. "I came by to tell you there's been another shooting in town."

"Anyone hurt?" Tate asked sharply.

"No, but Rider has a big hole in his helmet."

"Rider? He gave me a ride home the night I went out with Cheryl," Sutton butted into the conservation. "Is he okay?"

"You gonna give me a bowl of them beans?"

Before she could tell Greer where she would shove those beans, Tate answered her.

"He's fine. The son of a bitch is a Last Rider, and they each have nine lives."

"Thank God he wasn't hurt." Then another thought occurred to her. "When did it happen?"

"A couple of hours ago. Knox, his deputies, and the state police are swarming all over town, trying to find Tate."

"He couldn't have done it. He's been here with me the whole time."

"Whoever is doing the shootings doesn't know I'm here with you, or they would have waited for you to go into town," Tate stated.

"Is that good or bad?" Sutton asked, going to the oven to take out the cornbread. Lifting the heavy, cast-iron skillet, she placed it on the stove.

"Bad. It means either the fucker is getting ready to leave town, or…"

"Or?"

"He's about to escalate the attacks."

Sutton gave Tate a worried glance. "Knox said he would come back and arrest you if one more person was hurt."

"Knox knows Tate didn't do it. A witness gave a description of someone smaller than Tate running away down an alley."

"Then Tate's in the clear?"

"Not just yet. Knox sent the message to keep low. The state police aren't exactly willing to remove Tate from their suspect list, and they said the two killings might not be connected to Rider. They sent the bullet off to the state lab. It's going to be a few days before they can say if it's from the same gun that killed Helen Stevens."

Greer reached out to pinch off a large chunk of cornbread and popped it into his mouth. "Damn, I haven't had cornbread that good since Ma died."

"Have a seat at the table, and I'll fix you a plate." Sutton ignored Tate's amused gaze as she turned to the cabinet to take out plates and bowls.

She fixed both men heaping plates of food before placing them down on the table in front of them.

"What do you want to drink?"

"What do you think?"

Sutton went to the refrigerator, taking out the milk jug and placing it on the table with glasses. She had eaten at their home a few times before their parents had passed away and remembered how they liked to eat their cornbread.

She sat down after fixing herself a much smaller plate, enjoying watching the men eat the food she had cooked.

"I could fucking cry," Greer complimented. "They taste just like Ma's."

Sutton blushed with pleasure at Greer's compliment. "They should. She's the one who taught me how to cook them."

When the men were done eating, she watched as they each tore the cornbread up into their milk and ate it with their spoons.

"Never thought I'd say I would enjoy someone's cooking as much as Ma's." Greer's praise had her smiling.

She hadn't noticed how good-looking he had become before now. His features were more handsome than Tate's and more sculpted than Dustin's. His nose would benefit from a plastic surgeon. Sutton thought it looked like it had been broken more often than hers. His body was leaner than Tate's, but he was taller. Sutton could understand why the women in town would have trouble picking between the Porter brothers.

Tate's frown showed he wasn't happy with the way she was looking at Greer.

A fly suddenly flew by, and Sutton forgot about Tate's frown and became angry at herself for not lowering the screen after Greer had climbed through. The aggravating thing would drive her crazy until she managed to kill it. She was about to get a fly swatter when Greer's hand smacked down with the speed of lightning on the table, killing it. He used his fingers to flick it off the table then casually went back to eating his milk and cornbread.

Her eyes went back to Tate at his chuckle. "How am I looking now?"

"Better." Sutton laughed with him.

Greer looked at them suspiciously. "What?"

"There's soap and water over at the sink."

"Why, because I killed that little fly? I have an immunity to germs," he bragged.

Sutton thought for a second he was joking then realized he was serious.

"It's the truth. I'm never sick."

"I bet the others around you can't say the same."

"Nah, they're sick all the time."

"I wonder why," Sutton said sarcastically. She had a feeling Greer was a reincarnation of Typhoid Mary.

"Because I have my own elixir I drink every day. It keeps me strong and healthy as a horse."

"What's in it?"

"A cup of moonshine, a shake of red pepper flakes, half a lemon, and a clove of garlic. I haven't been sick in ten years."

"You eat a clove of garlic every day?" Sutton made a mental note not to stand too close to him.

"Yep. The moonshine kills the smell of the garlic."

"That's not all it kills. How long has it been since you had a date?"

Greer leaned back contentedly in his chair, patting his stomach. "Been too busy trying to find Lyle's murderer to go out lately."

"When you find him, give him that concoction of yours, and he'll beg to go to prison."

"Ha, ha. Very funny. That's the last time I share any of my recipes with you."

"You have others?" Sutton tried to hold back her laughter.

"Don't ask," Tate groaned. "Believe me, you don't want to know."

She couldn't help herself. "Come on. Share."

"I can get rid of a skin tag in a second."

"How?"

Greer reached into his pocket and pulled out a lighter, flicking it until a flame came up. "I burn the son of a bitch off."

Sutton cringed. "I don't have any."

"When you do, I'll take of it for you," he offered.

"I'll keep that in mind." She gazed at Tate to see if Greer was trying to pull her leg.

He shrugged. "I warned you."

"Yes, you did."

She decided she would take his advice. After all, Greer's approach to holistic medicine was frightening.

"I better go. I don't want to leave Logan and Holly alone for too long."

"Where's Dustin?" Tate asked sharply.

"He's keeping an ear out for gossip at Rosie's."

"Good idea."

Sutton watched as Greer took another piece of cornbread before climbing out the window again.

"Your brother needs help."

"He was just putting on a show for you."

"Why?"

"Because you were staring at him like a side of beef."

"I was not," she denied.

"You were."

Sutton remembered what Cheryl had told her about the brothers. "He was acting like a hillbilly because he thought I was attracted to him?" she asked in disbelief.

"Yep."

Sutton laughed so hard she had to hold her stomach. "I couldn't...ever...even if the world came to an end and he was the last man...be attracted to Greer."

"Why?"

"He's a mean jackass. He's obnoxiously rude, and—"

"He's a hillbilly?"

Sutton didn't miss the anger brewing in his eyes, and her laughter died. "I was going to say he probably sleeps with his gun in the bed. I'm a hillbilly, too, so why would you think I would say that?"

Tate snorted. "Technically, you're not a hillbilly. You lived in the fanciest house in town."

"I stayed every summer with Pap. I'm just as much a hillbilly as you and any other family living in these mountains."

"Is that so?"

"Yes!" Sutton snapped. Standing up, she angrily gathered the dishes, carrying them to the sink.

"Why are you getting so mad?" Tate came up behind her, putting his arms around her waist, his hands flattening against her stomach.

She stood rigidly against him. "Because these mountains are my heritage as much as they're yours. Pap and Granny lived on this mountain their whole lives, and their parents before them, for generations. My great, great, great-grandfather stole a chicken in Ireland so he would be shipped out with the other prisoners to come to America. He settled on this land, and every generation since then has lived and died on it. My father moved into town to live with my mother because Pap was still living, and he wanted his own home, but he would've moved back here after Pap died if he had left the house to him."

"Your pap knew you belonged here, and your father doesn't anymore. If this land means so much to your family, then why sell it?"

Sutton didn't answer his question.

Ignoring his grip around her waist, she started doing the dishes.

"Because I live nearby?"

She still didn't reply.

"Sassy pants, I'm going to get my answer."

"I haven't made my mind up yet," she finally admitted. "I was going to fix it up then decide."

"Then why did you go see Drake Hall?"

"I wanted to find out if he thought anyone would be interested in the property."

"You went to see him because you knew the first phone call he would make after you left his office was to me. You were sending me a message, whether you realize it or not."

Sutton turned around to face him. "I wasn't."

"You were." He stared down at her with an amused expression. Sutton gritted her teeth. "I was not."

"Okay." He lowered his head, placing a gentle kiss on her lips before she could jerk away. "Tell yourself that all you want. Do you want to know what I told Drake?"

Sutton had to admit to herself she did, so she nodded at him.

"I told him no, that I wouldn't buy it, and I would see to it that no one else bought it, either. I would make sure anyone thinking about buying it would have me as their crazy neighbor."

"Why would you keep anyone else from buying?" Sutton asked, hurt that he would sabotage her selling the land.

His hand went to the back of her neck, not letting her escape his piercing green eyes. "I knew he would tell you what I said. So, I sent back a message of my own: you weren't going to be leaving."

CHAPTER SEVENTEEN

"Tate..."

The indecision on her face almost had him backing away to give her more time. Instead, he caught her mouth with his, kissing her the way he had wanted to when they were in high school, but had been afraid of frightening her.

He slowly explored her mouth with the tip of his tongue before slipping inside. God help him, she still tasted the same, like the honey she had poured on her corn bread. He made sure not to crowd her against the sink as he reached around and turned off the running water, giving her his weight slowly as he pressed her backward so she could feel how she was affecting his body. The only way to realize they would be good together was to show he could give what she needed.

Truthfully, Tate had to admit to himself he had never been one to step back and hope what he wanted would fall into his lap. Hell no. If anything, what he wanted had never come easily. He had fought and worked hard to keep his family together. Sutton was going to become a part of his family. By hook or by crook, he *was* going to get this girl. If he had to use his body to do it, then he was okay with that.

He planted his hands on her hips, bringing her flush against his body, pressing his dick against the V of her thighs. Expecting her to stiffen, he was surprised when she melted against him, her arms circling his shoulders.

Delving into her mouth, he sucked her tongue into his, letting her take the lead, encouraging her with a moan. Boldly, she stood on her tiptoes to raise to his lips, he helped by lifting her onto the edge of the sink.

Her thighs circled his waist and her hands slid to sink her fingers into the thick mass of hair, holding him in. Her tongue teased his, sliding against his intimately, stroking the fire in his dick into a burning pain that was going to be hell to bank down.

Groaning, he lifted his head despite her trying to use his hair to tug him back to her mouth.

"Unless you're ready for me to carry you to your bed and fuck you, we need to slow down."

Her passion-filled eyes blinked up at him. "I thought you said we could go at my speed?"

"We can. That's why I'm giving you the option of stopping now." He teased the side of her neck. Sliding down, he brushed the top of her breast that was exposed by her T-shirt.

"I'm not ready."

"I'm cool with that." He lifted her down, placing her back on her feet before stepping back. "Want some help with the dishes?"

"Yes."

Tate went back to the table for the rest of the dishes. Then, taking a dish towel, he dried after she rinsed, placing them back onto the counter.

"Do you miss San Diego?"

"I miss the friends I made there. I went back to work at the pharmaceutical company, and I'm enjoying being back at work."

"That's good." Tate went quiet.

If she stayed in Treepoint, she wouldn't be able to keep her job. He didn't want to take away something else that was important to her. That had been done too often.

"Rachel works for The Last Riders."

"She told me when I had dinner with her and Cash."

"She's growing plants that can filter water."

Sutton quit washing dishes to stare at him. "That's interesting."

Tate nodded. "Maybe they could hire you to sell them. Or Dustin's an accountant. He's just starting out, but he was talking about hiring someone to watch the office and keep track of billing."

"Why are you telling me this?"

"So you know you have options." Tate continued drying the dishes without looking at her. "Treepoint is getting bigger, too. They're going to build a sporting goods store, and Dustin told me last week that Drake told him a nail salon is looking at the building next to the diner."

"It's good to know that, if I decide to stay, I can go out and buy a new fishing rod. I do my own nails." She lifted a soapy hand, showing him her unvarnished nails.

"Just thought I'd tell you," he grumbled.

"I think it's sweet the way you're trying to get me to stay, but a sporting goods store or a nail salon isn't going to be the reason. A job isn't, either. My company has a route in Kentucky. I would have to travel through the state, but that wouldn't bother me."

"It wouldn't?"

"No. If I wanted to stay, I could make it work."

"Good, and don't call me sweet. It might get out, and I'd have to kick someone's ass."

"I'll keep it just between us," she promised.

When they finished the dishes, he turned to go back into the living room, but her hand on his arm stopped him.

"Tate, I don't need you to fix me. I'm not broken."

He smacked her on the ass. "I can see that."

"Did you just smack my ass?"

He reached his hand out to cup her ass. "Do you need me to do it again so you can decide for yourself?"

"I can't believe you just did that. To a woman who's been physically abused, it could be traumatizing."

"You're the one who told me you weren't broken. You know I was playing. If you want me to walk on eggshells around you, tell me."

"Would you?"

"No, but I would try."

Sutton laughed. "At least you're honest."

"There you go." He slung an arm around her shoulder. "Let's watch some television."

Tate sat down on the couch, pulling her down next to him. He was about to reach for the remote when she snatched it up before he could.

"I'm not watching another episode of *Justice* or *Mountain Justice*."

"How about—?"

"I'm not watching *Moonshiners*, either," she cut him off, turning the channel until she came to the show she was searching for.

"Hell no, that isn't going to happen." Tate made gagging noises at *Naked and Afraid*.

"It's educational. If the world comes to an end, I'll know how to survive in the wilderness."

"If the world comes to an end, we won't be alive, and if we are, I'll hunt for us, but I'll guarantee I won't be buck-ass naked when I'm doing it." He tried to take the control from her.

"All right, all right, I'll change the channel." She flicked through the channels, coming to a stop.

Tate sat back, relaxing, recognizing *Duck Dynasty*.

"This okay?"

"I can live with it."

"Figures."

"What does that mean?"

"Rednecks and hillbillies are kissing cousins."

"That's not true." He propped his feet up on the coffee table.

"Yes, it is."

"Nope, hillbillies are smarter."

"I don't think they would agree with you."

"Yes, they would. That's why they're rednecks."

Sutton rolled her eyes. She managed to watch one episode, but when another reality show came on, she rose.

"I've got to go for a walk. My brain's going to turn to mush if I watch anymore."

"Hang on, and I'll go with you."

It didn't take him long to pull on his boots and grab his straw hat. Searching through the closet, he took out what he had been itching to do for the last week.

"I'm ready." Tate came out of the bedroom, carrying the fishing poles.

"We can't go fishing. Someone will see you."

"Get your keys. I know a spot where no one will bother us."

"All right."

They went outside after she retrieved her car keys. Once in the car, she turned to him.

"Where are we headed?"

"To Cash's house."

Sutton drove down the gravel driveway, turning in the direction of Cash's. It was just getting dark, but the drive didn't take long. When she parked in front of Cash and Rachel's home, Rachel ran out to greet Tate.

"You okay?" His sister stared up at him with worry.

"Everything's fine. Sutton and I were getting stir-crazy and thought we'd go fishing."

"You two have fun. Cash worked a double at the factory, or we'd join you."

"Rider doing okay?"

"Yes, he's lucky he was wearing his helmet. Usually, he doesn't wear one, but they were coming back from racing with Stud."

"Who's Stud?" Sutton asked.

"He's the president of The Destructors and The Bluehorsemen motorcycle clubs."

"His biker name is Stud? I need to see this guy."

Tate shook his head at her teasing. "You want to stay away from him."

"Why? Is he dangerous?"

"No, but his wife and her friends are," Tate told her, his hand going to Rachel to pull her to him. "How's the baby doing?"

"Good." His sister started to reach up and pat him on the chest, but Tate grabbed her hand.

"I'm fine. You take care of my niece or nephew."

"It's a girl," Rachel told him with a grin.

"Is Cash happy he's having a girl?"

"I haven't told him." Rachel laid her head on his chest, giving him a tight hug before taking a step back. "If you catch any extra fish, bring me one."

"Sure thing." Tate told his sister good-bye as he motioned Sutton forward into the woods.

The lightning bugs were just beginning to come out as they headed to the stream.

"I missed them." Sutton's voice was filled with wonder as she grabbed one of the small bugs, holding it gently in her closed hand before releasing it to fly again.

"I remember when I caught some in a jar for Rachel, and even though I put holes in the lid, you convinced her to let them go."

"I couldn't bear to see them trapped."

Tate thought of the irony that she had been too gentle to harm a bug then had found a monster to capture and torture her.

"What are we going to use for bait?"

Tate went to a tree. Picking up a stick, he dug around for a few seconds until he found a couple of worms and lifted them up to show Sutton.

She took the fat one wiggling in the palm of his hand. "You can have the skinny one." She pierced the squirming creature onto the hook.

"I dug it up. I should get the big one," Tate grumbled.

"I'll dig them up next time. I'll find two big ones."

"You always did try to one-up me."

She expertly cast her line into the water. "That's because you stop digging as soon as you find them. I keep looking until I find the one I want."

Tate cast his own line. "I hope you do that with men, too."

Chapter Eighteen

Sutton stared out at the rainy day, feeling as if she were about to climb the walls. Knox had stopped by the night before to tell them forensics should be back on the bullets today. If they came back that they were from the same gun, then he would officially clear Tate. That meant he would be going home either tonight or in the morning.

She put her hands in the back pocket of her cut-offs, rocking back and forth on the balls of her feet, counting to herself. Her counselor had told her it would ease anxiety from a stressful situation. It wasn't working. Her mind was debating why she should or shouldn't sleep with Tate.

Beginning a new relationship frightened the hell out of her, especially one that hadn't ended well the first time. He was being so gentle and attentive to her. She wanted to rub against him and beg him to fuck her. On the other hand, she had hated having sex with Scott. She had naively saved her virginity for the man she had planned to marry. Then, when she'd had sex with him, it had been the biggest let-down she had ever experienced. To be fair, she'd so looked forward to being with Tate that she didn't know if any man could have lived up to the expectations she set.

Her wedding night had been spent with Scott getting drunk at their wedding. In the hotel room, she had found herself on the bed with her wedding dress pulled up to her hips. It had been over before she had realized it had begun. If she hadn't felt the pain of his entry, she would have never known she'd had sex.

It had gotten steadily worse each and every time. She had tried everything to psych herself into making it a more enjoyable experience. It had taken the first beating Scott had given her to admit that she had made a mistake. She had blamed herself for the beatings, believing her lack of desire had driven him to act out in frustration.

The counselor had tried to convince her it was Scott, who had made no effort to arouse her, he had been the problem. Sutton had tried to convince herself over and over, but she knew the truth buried deep in her heart. She had never stopped loving Tate, so every time she'd had sex with Scott, she felt she was betraying that love.

Her finger drew a line down the foggy window.

"Want to watch some television?"

She didn't turn around when she heard Tate come into the room.

"No," she answered.

"Cards?"

"No."

"What do you want to do then?"

"I want you to leave me alone. Can I have some peace and quiet?"

"All you had to do was ask." His quiet voice had her jerking around.

"I'm asking. Okay?" She started to walk by him but he stepped in front of her, blocking her escape.

"What's wrong?"

"Nothing, Tate. I just want to be alone." Sutton ran her hand through her hair, dislodging the rubber band that held her hair back. Her hair tumbled down to her shoulders.

"Fine. If you don't want to tell me, then don't." He moved to the side to let her pass.

"Quit pacifying me as if I'm a damn child."

"Then quit acting like one," he snapped.

She wanted to hit out at him so badly she physically shook. She had to get out of the house, or she would do something she would regret. She turned on her heel, running out the front door as if the cabin was on fire.

"Sutton, it's raining!"

"Leave me alone!" she screamed back, taking off running, tears falling from her eyes that she couldn't hold back.

She didn't know how long she had run until she came to the tree Tate had found her at the last time she had taken off. Her arm circled the tree as she leaned against it, crying. If she had stayed, she would have begged him to make love to her, and she knew Tate well enough that he wouldn't let her go if she had. She wouldn't survive if they didn't make it this time around.

She stayed there until she was able to think straight, trying to figure out what would be the best decision for her. Not Tate or anyone else, just her.

Did she want Tate? Did she want him temporarily or just for the night? One question led to others just as difficult to answer. All the thinking she had been doing hadn't resolved anything, and she was cold and wet. The rain had plastered her hair to her head and drenched her clothes until her T-shirt and shorts clung to her body.

As she straightened from the tree, her eyes saw the edge of where the bark had been removed. Walking around, she noticed where she had scratched their names into the tree. He had teased her when she had done it.

Her hand went out to trace the initials, smiling when she saw what Tate had whittled into the tree just below their initials. "*4-ever.*" The marks were new.

Sutton headed home then, nearly slipping and falling several times with her determination to get back to the man who had left his mark, not only on the tree, but her heart. Like the tree, the mark wasn't going to disappear. It would be there until, like the tree, she was no longer standing.

She was halfway across the driveway when Tate came outside. He was wearing his boots and had put on a plaid shirt, leaving it unbuttoned, and his hat was on his head. Although he had tried to give her time alone, he looked like he had been about to come looking for her, exactly like he always would.

They were old friends and sweethearts. They couldn't get back what they had shared when they were younger. However, it was time for them to see if the adults they had become could make something more.

"Today's the seventh anniversary of Valentine's death," Sutton admitted as the rain poured down on her while she stared up at him. "I won't ever let another man hurt me again."

Tate stood at the end of the porch. Reaching up, he held the edge of the sloping roof, his shirt flapping in the soft summer breeze.

Her eyes dropped to his body, no longer feeling the cold rain as the temperature inside of her body rose.

"That's fair."

"You can stay here with me or go home. I'll leave that up to you."

"I'll be staying."

"So will I. I'm done running from you."

"Come here."

The demand in his voice had her putting one foot in front of the other until she found herself running up the steps toward him. She jumped up the last step, and he was waiting to catch her.

She plastered herself against him. "I don't want you to leave."

"I'm not going anywhere, and neither are you. I plan to keep you."

"You do?"

"I was stupid enough to let you go once, but I'm not going to make the same mistake twice." His hands cupped her ass, lifting her into his arms.

Sutton wrapped her legs around his waist, circling his broad shoulders. She loved his shoulders. He was strong, yet his strength didn't scare her, she felt protected and secure. Over the last ten years, she had proven she could survive the worst life could dish out. It was going to be nice to have someone strong enough to protect her if she needed help.

Tate slung open the screen door, carrying her inside the house. When he started to enter his bedroom, she raised her head.

"My room. I don't want to have sex on my pap's bed."

"Woman, it's not like he's here."

Stubbornly, she shook her head. "My bedroom."

"All right, but your bed's small. I'm going to get Greer to go into town and buy us a new bed."

"Don't you dare! I'll never hear the end of it. After Knox calls, we can go into town ourselves, and you can buy me dinner."

"Let's see how good you are first."

Her worries kicked in again at his playful attempt to tease her. Tate set her down on the floor beside the bed.

"You're soaking wet." His hands went to her waist, tugging her T-shirt over her head.

Sutton began to shiver, not because the room was cold, but because she was worried Tate wouldn't enjoy having sex with her. When he unsnapped her bra, she pressed herself against his chest so he couldn't get a good look at her breasts. Scott had complained they were too small and had wanted her to get a boob job.

Tate didn't slow down. Unsnapping her shorts, he pulled down them and her panties until all her clothes lay in a puddle at her feet. He then pulled away from her to take the clothes to the bathroom.

She jerked her robe on that was lying at the foot of her bed.

Tate came to a stop when he came back into the bedroom. "The idea was to take everything off, not to put more on." His eyes searched hers then lingered on her trembling fingers tying the belt in a knot at her waist.

"I was cold."

"Let's get you warm, then." He gave her a leering smile.

Sutton laughed, but it was cut off when his mouth covered hers and his tongue thrust into her mouth, not giving her a chance to think about being nervous.

He picked her up, laying her down on the middle of the bed.

"I like the way you kiss," she admitted.

Scott had never kissed her after they had married.

Tate threw his hat on her nightstand then jerked off his shirt. When he began to unzip his jeans, her nerves couldn't take it anymore.

"Wait!"

Tate paused, looking at her questioningly, and Sutton sat up, her hands unconsciously trying to tie the belt at her waist tighter.

"I'm not on the pill. We need to go into town to buy condoms."

Tate turned on his heels, leaving the bedroom again. He wasn't gone long before he came back with several foil packets in his hand, which he placed on the bedside table.

At her questioning look, Tate gave her a grin. "Greer put some in the bag he brought with my clothes."

"Isn't that convenient."

"I thought so." His hands went to his zipper again.

"I'm kind of thirsty."

He left again, coming back with a bottle of water then watching as she drank half of it before taking it and setting it on the bedside table.

Again, he went to remove his pants.

"Wait!"

Tate paused.

"Could we have some music?" She pointed at the old-fashioned radio on her dresser.

He went to the radio, fiddling with it several minutes before he found a station she liked.

"Anything else?"

"No...I think that's it." Sutton ran her trembling fingers through her wet hair, looking down at her lap as she listened to the sound of Tate removing his pants. She was going to disappoint him; she just knew it.

All the feelings of anticipation had disappeared, leaving behind a feeling of sick dread.

"Sutton...?"

She lifted her tear-filled eyes to his compassionate ones.

"I don't think I can," she admitted, keeping her gaze steady despite the gorgeous body that was wreaking havoc with her breathing.

Tate sat down on the bed next to her, reaching out to smooth her hair away from her face. "Are you afraid I'll hurt you?"

"No. I'm afraid I'll disappoint you, and you won't want me anymore," Sutton replied.

"What happens when we make love is only going to be a part of what makes our relationship a whole. If the rest of it is good, this will be, as well."

She nodded.

"You don't believe me?"

"I guess I do."

"Let me show you how good it can be. Trust me; I don't let anyone I love down."

He leaned over her, pressing her gently back into the soft mattress as he placed a kiss on her mouth that was achingly beautiful. The bedroom wasn't dark, but the only light came from the cloudy sky outside the bedroom window. The summer storm had turned into a drenching rain with lightning and thunder shaking the house.

"Are you afraid of storms?" Tate broke the kiss to whisper into her ear.

"No."

Tate got up from the bed to go to the window, shoving the curtains farther apart and raising the window until it was half-open before he came back to the bed to lie down next to her. He made no effort to touch her, just lying still next to her.

"What are you doing?"

"Waiting."

"For what?"

"For you to make love to me."

Sutton rose up, looking down at him wonderingly. Scott had always had her on her back or told her what to do. She didn't know how to take the initiative.

"I like to kiss."

"I do, too." His laid-back attitude gave her the reassurance no words could have.

Her mouth pressed against his and when he opened to her, she let her tongue slip inside, kissing him the way she had fantasized about during the dark years she had been alone. She brought her hands to his hair, holding on to him as his arms circled her waist.

At first, he let her take the lead until he tugged her to lie on top of him, and then he began to play and torment her with the flicks of his tongue. It was like 'catch me if you can'.

She rose up higher over him so she could get better access to him. Then she slid her hands down his chest, enjoying the feeling of the curly hairs there. Scott had waxed his sparse ones off. Tate's made her feel as if she had a man under her hands.

His hands went between them to untie the belt at her waist. Then he pushed the robe off her shoulders. His mouth went to her neck then brushed against her shoulders. She shivered as the lightning filled the room.

Her mouth went to his neck. An instinct she didn't know she possessed took over, and she bit down. His groan made her feel strong and possessive as she played with him.

"I'm leaving my mark on you."

He took one of her hands, placing it over his heart. "You did that a long time ago."

His admission removed her final misgivings and she lost herself in sensations as her hands slid over his body. Her lips traced down from his neck to his chest as his thigh parted hers, pressing upward until it rested against her pussy. Then he began to move it back and forth until it rubbed against her clit. An empty ache had her pressing herself down on his thigh.

Tate raised her slightly as he scooted himself up higher in the bed until his back was against the headboard. Sutton felt weightless as he held her hips in a tight grip, holding her poised over his cock. With exaggerated slowness, he lowered her until his cock nudged at the opening of her pussy, entering her in a way that had her holding her breath. Expecting the tight dryness she had always experienced before, she was surprised when Tate's cock slid easily into her as if they were made for each other. When he was completely inside of her, she arched, trying to take every inch of him.

"Take it easy," Tate soothed.

She had been unaware of the small whimpers of pleasure that had been escaping her.

"Don't stop!" she pled, wiggling herself on his cock.

He took the edges of her robe, pulling her face to his. "I'm not stopping," he growled. "Ride the storm, Sutton. Ride me."

She moved on him, his cock sliding in and out of her. The room illuminated with the lightning, and she wasn't sure if it was the thunder or her heartbeat that was increasing in intensity, driving her to frantically try to catch the eye of the storm before it disappeared.

He pulled apart her robe, taking her nipple in his mouth as she moved faster, her body spiraling into a series of explosions that had her feeling as if a thousand rockets were going off inside her body.

Tate shoved his cock higher inside her as he felt her clenching, making her soar again as she was about to come down to reality.

When she was able to focus again, she blinked, seeing Tate staring at her with a satisfied smile as he held her steady on him.

"For the first time in my life, I feel like a woman."

"Give me ten minutes, and I'll make you feel like a goddess."

Sutton laughed, dropping her head onto his chest. "I've laughed more in the last two weeks than I have in years."

"A man doesn't want to hear that when his dick is still in you."

Sutton laughed harder. "I think you can handle it."

"I can handle anything but losing you." Tate's expression turned serious. "I'm never going to let you go."

"Promise me." She snuggled more tightly against him, and his arms surrounded her. "Promise me you'll never let me go."

"I promise," he vowed.

For one blissful second, she allowed herself to believe him. She was sure, when he returned to his everyday life, he would get tired of her like the other women he'd had in his life over the years. But tonight, for now, Tate was hers.

The most painful lesson she had learned from Scott and losing Valentine was the present was all there ever was. If he changed his mind tomorrow, she would have the memory of this one perfect night. Therefore, she was going to toss her worries out the window and let tomorrow take care of itself.

Sutton glanced out the window and saw the rain had stopped, and the clouds were moving away.

"Tate, I see a rainbow." She pointed excitedly. It was practically outside their window.

"I do, too."

She glanced back at him. "You're not even looking."

"How could I not? I'm holding the pot of gold."

"That's so sweet."

"I've told you, I'm not sweet. Men don't want women to think of them as sweet."

"Okay...Now you're being an ass."

"That I can handle."

∞ ∞

"How much longer we have to wait here? I've got shit to do." Greer grumbled.

"Like what?" Tate didn't take his eyes off the door of the grocery store, he and his brothers had been waiting for over an hour. They weren't leaving until he sent a message, a strong one, not to fuck with him or his ever again.

"I don't know, anything's better than standing around twiddling my damn fingers waiting for her to come out. Why don't we just go inside and talk to her?"

"Because I want the bitch to get my message without anyone overhearing, I didn't keep my ass out of jail, just to have her put me there."

"Personally I like you better in jail, at least then you're not bothering me to do dumb shit like stand around here. I'm going inside, I'll give her the message for you."

Tate shoved Greer back nodding toward the entrance of the grocery store. "There she is." He stated grimly.

"Thank fuck. I thought I was going to have to break you two up, I didn't want to get my suit dirty. I've got a date tonight." Tate and Greer both turned to look at Dustin.

"You won't be getting any pussy tonight in that getup. Who you going out with?"

Tate paid only half attention to Greer as he picked on Dustin. "Kaley."

"Should have saved yourself the trouble of getting dressed up. She put's out to anyone who has a dick. She's older than you isn't she? She might be able to teach you a thing or two or three..." Greer smirked.

"Shut up...she doesn't hang out at the clubhouse with the Last Rider's anymore."

"That's only because they didn't let her join, doesn't mean she isn't still putting out to them at her place. Heard her and Cheryl need to both put a counter on their bedroom door to see which one of them is the biggest slut in town."

"I already know the answer to that. Diane has them both beat hands down." Dustin gave the killing blow to Greer's ego. "There isn't a pair of jeans in town that Diane's hands hasn't been down."

Greer punched Dustin knocking him backward into Tate who was fed up with the brothers riling each other.

"Cut it out!" Tate snapped, leaving them behind. He hadn't waited an hour to talk to her to miss the chance because of their squabbling. When Greer was bored he inevitably resorted to picking a fight to relieve his boredom. He didn't care who it was, as long as they would give him a good fight. Unfortunately it usually was his brothers because they were around each other so much, and they liked a good fight as much as he did. Because Dustin was younger and a dirty fighter who usually ended up kicking both their asses, while Tate and Greer were pulling their punches so as not to hurt their little brother. They were going to have to stop that shit, Dustin was ruthlessly taking advantage of it and was gloating afterward. Tate was going to put baby brother in his place one of these days, but first he needed to deliver a message.

Tate slammed his hand down on the car door before Lisa could open it.

"You don't want to say hi?"

The sound of fake laughter filled the air.

"I didn't see you, Tate. How have you been?"

"I've been better." Tate leaned back against her fancy sports car.

"Sorry to hear that, I heard the police were looking for you." Her eyes darted around the parking lot, Tate was sure she was searching for someone to help her escape. She was shit out of luck. Greer and Dustin had both positioned themselves out of view while Greer's truck kept anyone from seeing them from the other direction.

"That's all been straightened out."

"Oh."

"Don't sound so disappointed."

"I'm not, of course, I'm glad you've been cleared."

"Sutton's back in town." Tate controlled himself from strangling the lying bitch. "She told me that you said you were having my baby." Her expression became carefully blank as she opened her mouth to respond. "I would think twice about lying if I were you."

Her mouth snapped shut.

"I take it back, you're not as stupid as I thought you were. At least you aren't trying to lie your way out of it."

"I was pregnant." Lisa lowered her voice, so that only he could hear her.

"Maybe, but we both know it wasn't mine. Why blame it on me? That last night we were together you tried like hell to get me to fuck you without a condom, telling me you had it covered, that you couldn't get pregnant. That was the only piece of truth you spewed. You couldn't get pregnant because you already were, weren't you?"

"Yes." She admitted unable to look him in the eye. "I was pregnant, and the father refused to marry me, I thought if you had sex with me I could say it was yours. I knew you would marry me if you believed it was your child."

"You're right about that, there would have been no way a kid of mine would be raised alone with you." Tate snarled. "You underestimated my intelligence if you believed I would have fallen for that bullshit."

"I was young and didn't know what else to do. I'm sorry, I felt terrible right after I said that to Sutton."

"Not bad enough to fix it though were you? You've let her believe it for years."

Guiltily she remained silent.

Tate straightened from the car. "I'll thank God everyday for the rest of my life that I was fortunate enough not to fall into your trap. Because of you, Sutton and I lost years that we could have been together. You hurt her in ways you'll never know because I don't want you to have the satisfaction. You're damn lucky you're a woman, if you were a man I would shoot you dead where you stand."

Greer glanced over his shoulder. "I'll do it I don't give a fuck if she's a woman."

Tate ignored the tempting offer. "Instead I'm going to take away from you what Sutton lost."

Lisa's face turned a sickly shade of white. "What are you going to do?"

Tate reached into his pocket pulling out a photograph flinging it at her, uncaring of whether she caught it or not.

The photograph fell to the ground before she could catch it, she knelt reaching for the photo with trembling fingers. She stared at the picture before glancing back at him.

"What are you going to do?"

"I'm going to give that to the department of child protective services and make sure that pretty little girl you've been fostering is put in another home."

"Please, Tate, don't." No tears filled the calculating women's eyes, the only thing she was concerned about was how it would look to the town if she had the little girl removed from her home. She stood reaching out to touch his arm.

Tate jerked back out of her reach. "Be grateful, that's all I'm going to do. You should pray tonight and give thanks to God. If you ever dare to try to harm what's mine again, woman or not I'll make damn sure it's the last thing you ever do."

Tate nodded at the picture clutched in her hand. "You can keep that one, I have plenty more." Coldly he motioned for Greer and Dustin to leave, she stood, staring after him speechlessly as he strode to his truck. He waited for Greer to pull out of the parking lot before backing his truck up leaving Lisa still standing numbly by the car she was so proud of. She had always been too good to be seen in his truck, but not too good to pose for the pictures smoking weed and being fucked by two men at the same time with her husband watching. As he drove out of the parking lot he saw Shade sitting across the street on his big ass bike. Tate lifted two fingers to his hat tipping it forward in a salute. Shade nodded then started his bike, pulling out onto the street and accelerating out of sight.

Tate hadn't questioned why Shade had offered the photos, too happy for the opportunity for his revenge against Lisa. He had a feeling it was for the same purpose different reason. Either way, the little girl that Lisa was fostering had spent her last night under her roof. They may have been at cross purposes, but both had achieved their goal.

"Damn." He hated getting along with those fuckers, but for Sutton it had been worth the price of the weed he would be giving them for the next month. They had wanted two months free but Tate had Greer bargain them down after he had figured out they wanted the little girl away from Lisa.

Greer was a hell of a negotiator, he loved to argue, and he didn't care who he pissed off. Tate started whistling as he drove home. He really needed to put a stop to Greer's aggravating ways. He would get on it soon, but right now he was going home to Sutton. His hands curled over the steering wheel, gripping it tightly resisting the temptation to press down on the accelerator. Some things were too good to be true, and his life with Sutton made him realize how close he had came to never knowing true happiness. He had told her *if* was the most painful word in the dictionary and it was the truth. *If* she hadn't came back…*if* Lyle hadn't been murdered…*if* he hadn't listened when his heart had told him he loved her. He was done looking back. From now on, the only *if* he had left to deal with was *if* he could ever get his ring on her finger and finally claim what was his.

CHAPTER NINETEEN

"Run Logan! Don't let him catch you!" Sutton yelled, watching as Dustin chased after his son.

She laughed as Dustin grabbed Logan from behind, tossing him up into the air then deftly catching him. The squeals coming from Logan brought a smile to her face. She could watch the two together for hours, even if it amazed her that he was a father.

"They're just alike, aren't they?" she asked the woman sitting next to her at the picnic table.

"Yes." Holly grimaced. "Sometimes, I don't know who the child is."

"I bet you don't." Sutton picked up her beer, taking a drink as she studied the woman.

When Rachel had invited them over to hers and Cash's home for the Labor Day picnic, she had worried the police would be watching. However, after the sheriff had stopped by to talk to Tate, she had been relieved as she had unashamedly listened in as Knox had told Tate he had been officially cleared of killing Lyle, Mrs. Stevens, and shooting Rider.

"I handed over the bullets from your guns to the state police that Greer turned in to me. They didn't match the weapon used on the victims. An unregistered gun was used in both instances. The gun you hid, I took to Knox. It was bought at a gunshow, and the seller didn't pick out your picture as the buyer."

"You or the state police have no idea who it could be?"

"No. Jo let us search through Lyle's things. He was a drunk, but he didn't use drugs as far as we could tell. Helen Stevens wasn't, either, and all Rider does is what Shade buys off you."

"So, there's no connection between the three of them?"

"Nothing."

"Fuck."

"Yeah, it makes whoever is doing it damn near impossible to catch unless they make a mistake. It's freaking everyone in town out because no one knows who could be next. Keep an eye out. If you see anything, call."

"I will."

Sutton had seen the worried frowns on both men. Everyone in town was in danger until the killer was caught. The men had families they wanted to protect, but how could they do that with an invisible assailant?

Logan ran up to Holly. "Can I have something to drink?"

She reached into the ice cooler, taking out a bottled water and handing it to him.

"Thanks, Holly."

The pretty woman let the boy climb onto her lap.

"He's getting too big for that," Greer said, reaching into the cooler for another beer.

Sutton saw Holly throw him an icy look as her arms wrapped around the five-year-old little boy.

"No, he's not."

"You're going to make him a sissy."

"Do you even listen to the crap coming out of your mouth?"

Greer took a drink of his beer before responding to the angry woman. "It's the truth. If it wasn't for me, the boy wouldn't even know how to put his pants on one leg at a time."

"Holly, you're holding me too tight," Logan whined, jumping down off her lap when she loosened her hold.

"Go ask Aunt Rachel if she has any more grape salad," Holly urged him.

When he ran into the house, she glared at Greer. Neither tried to hide the antagonism between them. Sutton didn't know if she should intercede or get Tate, who was fishing with Cash.

"The only opinion that matters to me is Dustin's. Yours, fortunately, doesn't count."

"I've told Dustin that he needs to send your ass packing," he sneered.

"How's that working out?" she retorted.

"He said Logan's too attached for you to leave." Greer crushed the empty beer can in his hand. "I told him you're going to disappear, anyway, when your boyfriend gets out of jail next month."

Holly's face whitened, filling with hurt. Sutton remembered Tate telling her that Holly and her ex-boyfriend had broken into a law office to find out information on Logan's biological mother. Diamond hadn't pressed charges against Holly, but the ex had gone to prison.

"I haven't had any contact with Mitch, and I don't plan to. You know that. You're just being mean, Greer. I've apologized over and over for not going to the sheriff when Samantha died. I was trying to protect Logan."

"You were trying to protect your own ass."

Holly's tearful gaze shied away from hers. Sutton could tell she was embarrassed by Greer talking openly in front of her.

"Cut it out, Greer," Dustin said, coming out of the house and walking to stand behind Holly, placing a hand on her shoulder.

"She worked in Diamond's office for months. I've told you not to trust her, little brother. You're going to find out the hard way that she's a snake in the grass." Greer reached into the cooler for another beer.

"That's your third one," Holly spoke up when he opened it and took a drink.

He raised a brow at her, drinking all of it then crushing it in his hand again.

"You should have one. You might actually learn how to have a good time."

"I'll pass."

"Thought you would. You couldn't loosen up if you had a six-pack."

"If you're so interested in me having a good time, why don't you leave? That would make my day."

Greer's mouth snapped open. From his expression, his reply was going to be ugly.

"Don't do it," Dustin warned. "I'm getting tired of the way you treat Holly. You don't have the right to throw her breaking into Diamond's office in her face when you were the one who planted that evidence on Knox to take the suspicion off me when Samantha died. We all made mistakes."

"Mine didn't involve kid-snatching."

Holly stood up with Logan's bottled water in her hand. Sutton gaped as she flung it in Greer's shocked face. He started toward her, but Dustin blocked him.

"Settle down. You deserved it."

Greer pointed his finger at Holly. "One day."

"I'm *sooo* scared. You big ape, why don't you go get your caveman club and scratch your ass with it? That is, if you can find it. Let me show you where it is." Holly was shaking in fury as she reached out to pat his cheek.

Sutton admired her for standing her ground against the formidable man.

Greer nearly knocked Dustin down trying to reach Holly. They barreled into the picnic table, and Rachel flew out of the house with a gun in her hand.

Sutton hastily jumped up from the picnic table, ready to scream her lungs out in terror when Rachel took aim, firing it at Greer. Stunned, she could only watch as bright yellow paint exploded on Greer's shoulder.

"Shit! That hurt, Rach..." Greer practically fell, trying to move away from Dustin when Rachel shot another paintball at him, hitting him on his butt as he turned to run.

"He should be able to find his ass now, Holly."

The two women burst into laughter while Greer remained silent, too wary of getting shot at again.

Logan came out of the house. "Can I go next, Aunt Rachel?"

"No!" Greer stormed off toward the river.

"Sure. Come on. I've got a target set up on that tree over there."

"Do you think that's a good idea? I really don't like him playing with guns."

This time, Holly got a reaction from both Rachel and Dustin.

"It's a paintball gun, and there hasn't been a Porter born who hasn't learned to shoot the eye out of a squirrel at fifty feet."

Sutton and Holly both blanched at Rachel's bragging.

"Is she joking?" Sutton asked Tate as he and Cash returned with a string of fish.

Greer remained out of range of the paintball gun.

"No," Tate and Cash both answered at the same time.

"Logan is not going to shoot the eye out of a squirrel," Holly said empathically.

"I don't want to shoot a squirrel." Logan's bottom lip began to tremble, and his eyes brimmed with tears.

"Don't worry, baby; no one's going to make you." Holly picked the little boy up, patting him on his back.

"See? I told you she's making a sissy out of him," Greer yelled from across the yard.

"Logan, go inside and get yourself a freezy pop out of the freezer. I'll be there in a minute."

"She's gonna make him fat, too!" Greer's loud mouth made Sutton cringe.

Holly set Logan back on his feet, waiting until the door closed behind him before turning to Rachel, holding out her hand.

"Give me the paintball gun."

"Why?" she asked suspiciously.

"Because I'm going to show him who the sissy is."

Rachel took a step back, holding onto the gun. "I don't think that's a good idea. You might hurt him."

"That's the plan."

"Give her the gun," Tate ordered.

"Are you serious?" Rachel questioned her older brother.

"Yes, but give him a minute to get a head start." Tate looked over at Greer. "Run."

Greer took off like a pack of wild dogs was after him when Rachel reluctantly handed Holly the paintball gun. She shot off a couple of balls at him, barely missing the fleeing man. Tate, Cash, and Dustin burst out laughing at Greer.

Sutton shook her head at the nutcases surrounding her when even Rachel began to urge Holly on. Mumbling to herself, she decided to join Logan inside.

"Where are you going?" Tate called out.

"Inside."

"Why?"

"To show Logan that normal people do exist."

"We're normal!"

"There are people in mental institutions more normal than you all are."

"Don't be that way." He came to her side, slinging his arm around her shoulder. "We're just having some fun."

Sutton rolled her eyes at him. "You're all setting bad examples for him. What if he grows up to shoot at people and fight all the time?"

Tate's chest puffed up proudly. "Then he'll be a Porter."

"And that's a good thing?"

"Could be worse. He could be a Hayes or a Coleman."

Sutton turned to Holly who had quit shooting when Greer had finally managed to get out of her sight.

"Give me the gun." She held out her hand toward Holly.

Tate's arrogant smile slipped when Holly handed her the paintball gun, and she then trained it at Tate.

"Who's laughing now?"

℘ ℭ

"Are you still mad?" Sutton had suffered Tate's stony silence all evening after she had brought the paintball gun home at Cash's urging. It seems the man didn't want the weapon around if he pissed Rachel off.

She took off her robe and laid it on the chair beside the bed. Placing a knee on the mattress, she prepared to climb into the bed.

"That last shot was unnecessary, and it hurt like fuck."

"You shouldn't have tried to take it away from me. You were supposed to run." Sutton's eyes shied away guiltily from the bruise on his side.

"A Porter doesn't run."

"Greer did," she reminded him.

"We think he was adopted."

Sutton couldn't help falling onto the bed, laughing. "What about the red hair?"

"It's more brownish red."

Sutton traced her fingers over the bruise then leaned over him, placing a gentle kiss on the angry mark. Tate settled himself, getting more comfortable against the pillows.

"That make it better?"

"Not yet," he answered grumpily.

Sutton ran the tip of her tongue over it.

"That's helping a little."

She slid her lips to the right to the faint mark on his stomach. "Better?"

"Getting there," he groaned.

Sutton tugged down the blanket that was covering his lower body, and then she delicately flicked her tongue against the flesh at his hip, moving down to the mark on his thigh, gently brushing the edge of her teeth over the mark she had left there.

"You're missing the spot that's really hurting." He wrapped his hands in her hair, trying to guide her toward his cock that was straining upward.

"I don't remember shooting you here." Sutton traced the tip with her tongue before taking the head into her warm mouth.

"Every time you look at me, it's like a shot to my dick." His hand went to the nape of her neck, holding her in place as his hips surged upward, forcing her to take more of his cock into her mouth.

She sucked on him, feeling him get harder and longer in her mouth. She had only given Scott oral sex a couple of times, disliking having him in her mouth. With Tate, she couldn't get enough.

Relaxing her throat, she tried to take more of him, wanting him to enjoy it more than he had with other women. She felt herself dampen at the empty feeling in her pussy and pressed her thighs together to lessen the ache.

"Let me help with that."

Tate rolled to the side, flipping her upside-down. His intention had her scampering to the edge of the bed.

"I'm not ready for that. I've never...Scott wouldn't..."

Tate sat up, the passion in his eyes deepening. "Come here. You're making me horny as hell."

"Not tonight...Maybe some other—"

Sutton squealed when Tate took her ankle in a firm grip, dragging her down the bed. Her thighs splayed open inelegantly, and without giving her time to protest, his mouth latched on to her pussy. Sutton arched. Any protest she was about to give died instantly at the unbelievable pleasure of having him tease her clit with his tongue.

Rolling to her side, she took him back in her mouth, wanting to share the pleasure he was giving her. Squeezing his balls in the palm of her hand, she found a rhythm that mimicked his flicking tongue. The more Tate tormented her, the more she tormented him, each trying to outdo the other as their slick flesh slid against each other.

Sutton raised her head briefly, trying to catch her breath as she rested on his thigh. She moaned as she desperately tried to keep herself from coming. Turning her head to the side, she bit down on the inner flesh of his thigh.

A loud groan had her rising to take his cock back in her mouth as she gave up trying to hold back, giving her orgasm full reign as she brought Tate to his by sucking the tip of his cock, her hand sliding slickly on him as he gave up his own battle.

When he finished, Sutton dropped back onto the bed, panting as she stared up at the ceiling.

Tate's voice was hoarse when he asked if she was all right. When she was unable to answer, he changed position, laying his head down next to hers at the bottom of the bed.

"Sutton?"

Her head tilted to the side. "I'm not frigid."

Tate's mouth turned into a smirk. "Darlin', you don't have a frigid bone in that sexy body of yours." He plucked at her still-pebbled nipple.

"I thought I was for years."

"If you were married for years, and he never went down on you, then he was an idiot." His mouth went to whisper in her ear, "Get used to it. I could get addicted to the taste of you."

"Did I do okay? I know I'm not very good, but I'll get better. Scott always complained I was too rough."

"He was a sissy, wasn't he?"

Sutton tried to crawl over him to get out of the bed. When Tate had moved his things into her bedroom, he had shoved the bed against the wall, telling her they would get more fresh air at night.

"Where are you going?"

"To get the paintball gun."

CHAPTER TWENTY

"You're getting all dressed up just to meet your boss?" Tate sat on the bed, pulling on his boots.

Sutton sighed. "For the fifth time, he's my boss, and I don't wear jeans and a T-shirt to work."

"You're not going to work; you're meeting him for lunch."

"To talk about the routes I'll be taking over, which is work," she stressed.

"Ready?"

"I already told you I didn't need you to drive me into town. I'm driving myself."

"You sure?"

"I'm sure." She brushed past him, going to the living room to pick up her purse.

"Be careful and keep an eye out for anything strange. Remember, they haven't found the shooter."

"I'll be careful." She stood on her tiptoes to kiss him good-bye. "I won't be long."

"Okay."

Tate buttoned up his shirt and pulled on his hat before going to the porch, hearing the motor of Sutton's car grind. She tried several times to turn the motor over before getting out of the car.

"Having a problem?" Keeping a straight face with effort, he saw the suspicion in her eyes.

"The car won't start."

"Let me have a look." He casually walked over to the car. Pressing a button by the steering wheel, he popped the hood and raised it, leaning over the engine and studying it before twisting a few wires, and then he straightened. "It's dead."

"I knew that."

"Well, it's really dead. Would you like me to give you a lift to town?"

"Yes, please. I don't have time to call someone else for a ride."

"You sure?" he asked nonchalantly.

"I'm sure." Her jaw was clenched tightly as she walked toward his truck, nearly tripping in her high heels.

"Be careful. It hurts like a bitch to fall on gravel."

He took a quick step backward when she slung the truck door open, nearly hitting him.

"Whoa! There's no need to be so pissy." He climbed behind the steering wheel, starting the truck.

"Tate, I know damn well you had something to do with that car not starting."

"It's a rental, so what can you expect? I remember one time I had to rent a car, and it broke down—"

"Shut up," Sutton growled.

Tate closed his mouth, humming "Camp Town Ladies" all the way into town. By the time he pulled into King's restaurant, he thought she was going to explode.

As soon as he parked, she jumped out of the truck, and Tate moved to get out.

"Don't you dare, I'll get Liam to drive me home."

"I can wait."

"Tate Porter..."

He lifted his hands up in surrender, shutting his truck door. He grimaced when she slammed her door shut.

"I'm going to need a new truck with the way you're treating it," he yelled out his window to her retreating back. He smiled when she practically tore the door to King's restaurant off the hinges.

Whistling, he strummed his fingers against the steering wheel, giving her several minutes to get settled before he slid out of his truck, not bothering to lock it. No one in town would be stupid enough to steal his truck. They could find a better one in the junkyard.

It didn't take him a second to find her in the busy restaurant.

The owner of the restaurant walked toward him with a cold expression on his harsh face.

"You eating or drinking?" King blocked him from entering the restaurant any farther.

His brows drew together. "Is that any way to greet a customer?"

"Depends on whether you're eating or drinking and if those brothers of yours are joining you. The last time you came in with Greer and Dustin, one waitress quit, and I had to fire another one."

"How is it our fault she kept giving us free beer? And Lindy shouldn't have believed Dustin was really going to pay her bills and set her up so she would never have to work again. He was drunk off his ass. She should have at least waited until he sobered up to quit."

King's jaw clenched. Tate could tell his explanation was only making the hard feelings worse.

"It's just me today. I'm here with my woman." He nodded toward Sutton and a slickened-up man sitting in a booth. Sutton's back was to him, and her boss's attention was pinned on her.

"Since when do you have a woman?"

"Are we going to stand here all day, shootin' the shit, or are you going to let me eat lunch?" he asked, not answering the snide question.

King waved his hand toward Sutton's table, stepping to the side so he could pass.

As Tate casually walked toward her table, her boss's eyes widened.

When he reached the side of the booth, he gave Sutton a fake smile. "I got tired of waiting in the truck."

Sutton's mouth dropped open.

Taking advantage of her surprise, he slid into the booth next to her, forcing her to scoot or get moved over. Wisely, she gave him the room to sit next to her.

"Uh…I thought you had left."

"Nah, I was hungry."

Her eyes narrowed on his coming-off-as-a-hick attitude.

"Tate, this is my boss, Liam Allen. Liam, this is Tate Porter, a friend of mine."

"Boyfriend," Tate corrected her, taking the menu out of her hand before she decided to use it to hit him.

"It's nice to meet you." Liam held out his hand to him. Tate reached out to shake it, the two men sizing each other up. "So, you're the reason Sutton's decided to move back to Kentucky?"

Tate placed his arm on the back of the booth, drawing a reluctant Sutton closer. "Good thing. I don't see me and California as a good match. It's hot as shit there."

"You were going to move to California if she didn't move back?"

"Yes."

"You were?" The anger in her eyes disappeared at his claim.

"Of course. She's mine, and I want her to be happy," Tate said truthfully, frowning when he saw tears brimming in her eyes.

His hand went to the nape of her neck, gently soothing her. She sank against his side and Tate leaned down, brushing his mouth against hers. It was the first public display of affection he had ever given a woman, showing without embarrassment how much he was into her.

"I can see you both are a good match. I'm happy for you, Sutton." The sincerity in Liam's voice eased the jealousy in his gut.

There was no comparison between them. Liam was sophisticated, handsome, and charming. Tate knew, side by side, he had the short end of the stick in all three categories.

The waitress took their order, leaving them alone again.

Tate listened silently, letting them talk about her schedule. Sutton would be traveling two or three days a week to nearby cities, allowing her to be home by a reasonable time. She would be driving out of town only two days a month, which would require her to be gone overnight. Tate thought about informing her that she wouldn't be spending those nights alone—he would be traveling with her—but decided he would let her find that out on her own. He didn't want her to think he was being pushy. He was; he just didn't want her to figure it out too soon. She would find that out the day she left for one of those trips.

She had her own surprise in store for him when they parted with her boss in the parking lot.

"I'll see you next month when I drive out to get my car and pack up my apartment."

Liam shook his hand after saying good-bye to Sutton.

"Take care of her. I can't tell you how good it is to see her so happy."

Damn, Tate hadn't anticipated liking the man. There were very few men he could actually stand.

Tate made an offer he made to only a few. "Come for a visit some time, and I'll take you hunting."

"I might take you up on that. What kind of game do you hunt? Bear?"

"Hell no, they're mean fuckers. We can hunt for squirrels and possums. I have one that's getting in our trash. I'm going to kill that little bastard. Might not wait for you to come back to get rid of him."

Liam burst out laughing. "Don't wait. I imagine that can be aggravating."

"It is. Sutton talked me into catching him and setting him free somewhere else, so I took him to The Last Riders' clubhouse and let him go. Little bastard found his way back a week later, though. Looked half-starved to death. They don't have good trash…"

Sutton tugged on his arm. "Liam wants to leave. We're holding him up."

"Not at all. I'm enjoying this. There's a motorcycle club here? This town doesn't seem the place a club like that would make home."

Tate snorted. "They love it here and have stolen all the good women in town but one." He jerked his head toward Sutton. "I managed to catch her. I always knew I was smarter than them," he bragged.

"I'll let you know when I can take a few days off from work so you can take time off from work—"

"Don't worry about that. I'm my own boss."

"Really, what do you do?"

Tate's eyes narrowed on him. "You a Fed?"

Sutton's elbow struck him in the ribs. "We need to go. Bye, Liam." She grabbed Tate's arm, trying to push him toward his truck.

"I'm a pharmacist and businessman," Liam continued like Sutton hadn't said anything. "A federal agent isn't one of the many jobs I've held."

Tate spat on the ground. "Me, neither."

Sutton's face turned red and her eyes promised retribuation.

"So, what is it you do?"

Tate shook off Sutton. The woman was about to rip his arm out of its socket.

"I'm a pharmacist and a businessman, like you. You do your work in an office or a lab; I do mine in a field. I grow medicinal plants."

The interest in Liam's eyes deepened. "I've never met anyone who actually grows the components of medicine. Which plants do you grow?"

"Weed."

"Weed?"

"You sure you're not a Fed?"

"Tate!"

Sutton's boss burst out laughing. "I'm sure. I've even been known to take a hit every now and then."

Tate sniffed the air. "I'd say a few hours ago."

Sutton's hand dropped from his arm. "Liam, please don't fire me. He's not my boyfriend. Actually, he's barely an aquantanice—"

Tate raised his brow at her. "Who was that in my bed last night, then? It sure as hell looked like you when you were—"

"Shut up!" she hissed.

"It's all right, Sutton," Liam interrupted the squabbling couple. "I'll definitely be back in a couple of months. I'll be interested in trying your product."

"Don't you dare ask if he's a Fed again," Sutton threatened.

"Wasn't going to," Tate said indignately. "You have offices in Colorodo?"

"Actually, yes."

"I have a couple of plants for you to take. You could pass them off to a cooperative that grows the plants. I have one I developed when a friend of my cousin's mother was diagnosed with cancer. Seemed to help her out quite a bit before she passed away."

"I'd be glad to pass them along."

"Can't give you more than a couple because they'll say I'm distributing, but if you give them to a good grower, he'll know what to do with Kentucky Gold."

"You named it?" Sutton asked.

Tate almost reminded her that she had wanted him to quit talking, but he didn't want to sleep on the couch tonight. His woman had a temper when riled.

"Had to. I developed it. I wasn't going to have some other fucker naming it something stupid."

Liam opened his car door, asking, "Why Kentucky Gold?"

"Wait until you try it. Nothing compares. Not even that fake shit the Colemans are selling. I could sell it all day long, but I only grow what I give to the people in town who need it."

"Why not sell to everyone?"

"Because it would sell so fast I wouldn't have enough for those who need it. My regular customers act like they've got a tick up their ass when I tell them I run out. It's easier not to let them know what they're missing out on."

Liam finally turned to Sutton. "Sutton, I could take a long weekend in a couple of weeks and drive your things up here to you."

"I wouldn't want to impose—"

"No imposition. I'll take a rental car back."

"If you're sure…"

"I'm sure. Some friends are worth their weight in gold." He winked.

☯ ☯

While Sutton remained silent on the drive home, he wondered what he had said or done that had pissed her off the most.

"Did you really mean that you would have moved to California?" Her soft question had him cutting her a quick glance.

"I don't say shit I don't mean," he told her as they got nearer to Rosie's bar. "Want to stop in and get a beer?"

"I'd like that. I haven't seen Mick since I've been back."

Tate turned into the parking lot. As usual, there were plenty of bikes parked there, and Greer's truck was parked in his usual spot. When he spotted the large, black Chevy truck, he almost turned around to leave, but he couldn't bring himself to leave Greer without back-up, even if the stupid fucker was stupid enough to stay with The Last Riders and the Hayeses there.

Parking, he turned off the truck. "Stay by my side. There might be trouble."

She shocked the shit out of him when she gave him an anticipatory grin. "Really, who with?"

"The Hayeses. Greer won't pick a fight with The Last Riders. We owe them for fixing me up and Knox not turning me in. The Hayeses are always looking for trouble, and Greer likes to give it to them."

"Why doesn't he like the Hayeses? They were always nice to me, even though we only saw them during football and basketball seasons," she said, sliding out of the truck and slamming the truck door.

Tate waited for her at the front of his truck, holding out his hand. A warm feeling struck him when she immediately placed hers in his.

"Jessie was as good in sports as her brothers."

"You aren't their biggest competition in the county," he answered.

The Hayeses were the most clannish in town, keeping to themselves even when it came to school. The two brothers and one sister were allowed to participate in the school's sports activities, but remained homeschooled until they graduated.

"Jessie should be; they treated her just like one of the boys, and still do. She can out hunt and out shoot them, and she wouldn't wear a dress if someone threatened her life."

"She's sweet," Sutton argued.

"That's what you said about the possum, and it nearly ripped my arm off when I set it loose."

He held the door open for her to enter the bar. It was already filled, though it was still early. He saw Greer standing at the bar with his hand on Diane's ass. The local woman was the biggest slut in town. She was constantly promising Greer he was the only one she was seeing, and inevitably, she would be found out to be lying when one of her lays would brag to Greer. He was constantly getting in fights and paying out for the damages the fights caused. Tate was getting damn sick of bailing him out of jail over the lying bitch.

Greer grinned at him when he and Sutton took the bar stools next to him. "You finally decide to come out and have some fun?"

"Been having plenty at home."

Greer gave Sutton a smirk. "My brother keeping you busy?"

"Watch your mouth," Tate warned his brother. He could tell from the dazed look in his eyes he had already had one too many beers.

Greer held his hands up in the air. "Didn't mean any disrespect. Sorry, Sutton."

"It's okay—"

"No, it's not," Tate cut in. His brothers were going to treat Sutton right, even if he had to knock the hell out of them.

"I've been waiting for Greer to pick a fight with someone. Didn't expect it to be his own brother," Mick quipped, coming to stand in front of them behind the bar.

"Hi, Mick," Sutton broke in, diverting the tension between him and his brother.

"Heard you were back in town. Good to see you, girl."

She gave him a sweet smile that, if Tate didn't know Mick wasn't interested in her, would have made him jealous. He had only seen that particular smile a couple of times, and he wasn't ready to share it with anyone else.

"What have you been up to?" Mick opened a couple of beers, placing them down in front of them.

As Sutton described her life in California, Tate noticed the Hayeses studying her from across the bar. He caught their eyes, giving them a silent warning.

"Been a while since we've had a good fight," Greer said, seeing where he was staring.

"We're not going to have one tonight. Sutton's here."

"Good luck with that," Greer said, getting off his stool. "Let's go dance." He took Diane's hand, leading her toward the dance floor.

Tate thought it wasn't a bad idea. When Mick moved away to wait on his customers, he turned to Sutton.

"Feel like dancing?"

"What do you think?" She jumped down from her stool, eagerly taking his hand. The woman used to love to dance when they had dated in high school. Mick was nice enough to let them sneak in the bar and dance for a few hours before it became crowded. He had never served them liquor, only gave them a place to hang out on a Saturday night.

Sutton slid her arms around his neck, pressing against him as the music turned slow. His hand went to her ass, securing her against him, and her head fell to his shoulder. Tate thought it was the most perfect moment he had experienced in his life. He didn't want it to end, even when the music switched to a different song with a faster beat. Still, they didn't move, staying pressed against each other, neither wanting the moment to end.

Tate stiffened with her in his arms when he felt a hand tap him on his shoulder.

"I'm cutting in. Pretty girl like her needs to dance with someone who knows how."

Tate didn't budge. "Go find your own woman to dance with. This one's taken."

"What does she have to say about that? Maybe she wants to dance with me."

His jaw clenched.

Sutton raised her head. "He's right; I'm taken."

Tate's chest swelled with pride.

Asher's eyes went to Sutton's hand that rested on his arm. "Sorry, Tate. I didn't realize you had gotten married."

Instantly, he understood that Asher had seen the wedding band on her hand.

"We're not married."

"Didn't know the Porters fucked around with married women."

He felt Sutton tense in his arms, expecting him to punch Asher.

"She's a widow."

The smirk on Asher's face disappeared. "Sorry."

Sutton nodded, and Asher moved off onto the crowded dance floor.

"I'm shocked that you didn't hit him."

"Nah, I'm not letting that asshole get to me tonight. I'm having too good a time."

She relaxed back against him. "Me, too." He barely heard her whisper over the loud music.

When the other couples on the floor kept bumping into them, Tate led her back to the bar. He suspected Greer was still dancing with Diane, but he couldn't see him among the crowd.

Holt was dancing with Reva, a woman Tate had occasionally fucked on and off for the last couple of years. He hadn't been with her in the last eight months since she had started hinting at him that she wanted a ring. They came off the dance floor and sat down next to them at the bar.

Tate finished his beer. "Ready?"

Sutton nodded.

"You're not leaving, are you, Tate? I thought we could dance."

"No, thanks, Reva." He took a twenty out of his wallet, laying it down on the bar to pay his tab.

"Come on...Don't leave. Holt can keep her company until you get back."

"Don't want another of Tate's leftovers," Holt spoke as Tate gave Sutton his hand to help her down. Tate's hand dropped.

Jerking around to face Holt, he made himself give the man a chance. "I don't give a fuck if you insult Reva—she's not my woman—but keep your mouth off Sutton."

"Don't want my mouth on her. The way you two were acting on the dance floor, my dick would rot off if I fucked her. Heard Cheryl's picked up the clap and been giving it out. Since you were with her a couple of months back, maybe Sutton should be getting herself checked out."

Fury exploded in Tate's head. The Porter temper was notorious throughout Treepoint. It was actually hardest to rile in Tate. Most of the fights he found himself involved in were because he enjoyed fighting.

With blinding fury, his fist swung out, landing a punch on Holt's stomach. He fell back, knocking over barstools as the customers hastily moved out of the way.

"You son of a bitch!"

Tate didn't give Holt time to recover before swinging his fist again, but it was caught midair by Asher who shoved him against the bar.

"Don't fucking touch my brother!" Asher reached for the beer bottle he had finished, about to bash it against his skull, but Sutton grabbed his arm.

"Leave him alone."

"Stay out of this, Sutton," Tate ordered. He didn't think the brothers would stoop low enough to touch her, but he wasn't willing to take the chance.

Before Asher could make another move, Greer was there, jerking Asher away from Tate and Sutton. It took two seconds before the men began laying into each other. At the same time, Asher had gathered enough air in his oxygen-deprived lungs to come back for more. The two men fell onto the table next to the bar, knocking the customers and drinks out of the way.

Tate felt Asher land a lucky punch on his eye before he could put him in a stranglehold.

"That's enough!" Mick yelled out, coming from behind the counter.

A couple of The Last Riders pulled Greer off Holt, who was steadily gaining momentum and was threatening to twist Greer's arm off. Greer swung his arm back, trying to knock Rider off him.

"I'm trying to help your drunk ass." Rider barely managed to let go of Greer before he succeeded in hitting him.

"I don't need your help."

"That isn't what it looked like to me," Rider mocked Greer, angering Tate.

"We can handle this ourselves." Tate kicked Asher in the balls, forcing him to his knees.

"No skin off my nose. I wasn't in the mood for a fight tonight, anyway." Rider and Train moved away, leaving them alone to deal with the Hayeses.

Tate reached down, jerking Asher's head up with his hand in his hair. "I'm getting tired of you two fucking with us. Do it again and Jessie is going to be looking for your bodies for the rest of her life."

Holt wiped the blood from his mouth with his hand. "Big talk from a man who hid behind a woman to keep from going to jail."

Tate went for him, but stopped when Sutton tugged on his T-shirt. "I'm ready to go home."

Tate stopped, seeing the concern she didn't try to hide. He turned back to Holt. "Next time," he promised.

"I'm shitting my pants," Holt mocked.

Tate waited until Greer found Diane so they could leave together. Diane got behind the wheel of Greer's truck after he climbed in.

His brother hung out the window as he said, "We whipped their asses."

"Drive him into town with you, Diane, and keep him overnight. He'll wake Logan up going into the house."

She gave him a seductive smile. "You two want to come and have a drink at my place?"

"We'll pass." Sutton tugged him away from the truck.

"I wasn't going to accept," Tate said as they watched Greer's truck pull onto the road. "Who were you trying to get away from?"

"It was a tie," Sutton answered as he opened the truck door.

He climbed in the truck, taking her hand back in his and linking their fingers together. He tugged her closer until she sat next to him. Then Tate drove out of the parking lot, but instead of turning in the direction of home, he made a right, turning back toward town.

"Where are we going now?"

"I thought we would take a detour before going home."

She started giggling when he made a left a mile down the road.

He expertly guided the truck up the mountain until they reached the top. Tate parked the truck, looking out over the mountains.

"I haven't been up here in years." He shifted until he could look at her. "Not since I was here with you. I remember coming up here after we went to Rosie's. Every time we came, I hoped to get past first base with you."

Sutton reached out, unbuttoning his shirt. "Get ready. You're about to hit a homerun."

Chapter Twenty-One

Sutton smoothed her hands over Tate's chest. God, she loved touching him. Every touch reminded her she was with him, that it wasn't a dream.

She placed a kiss at the base of his throat, her tongue exploring the salty taste of him. "When you used to touch me, it was everything I could do not to give in to you. Now I can't imagine not having you inside me."

His hand went to the hem of her dress, shoving it out of the way before sliding his hand up her thigh and going to her pussy. "If I could go back in time, I would beat the shit out of Cash and drag you into my truck. You would have broken and told me the truth. You never could hold back with me."

"That isn't true. I didn't have sex with you."

"Only because I didn't push you."

Sutton had to admit to the truth in that statement. Tate had always let her make up her own mind.

A tear ran down her cheek at the thought. He had set an example for what she should have seen was a flaw in Scott's behavior before they were married. It always had to be Scott's way. Even when they were picking out the decorations for their wedding, he had done the choosing. She had ignored the warning signs and had paid the price, and so had Valentine. That was what she had found was the hardest to deal with.

"Look at me, Sutton."

She raised her head to stare into his eyes and caught her breath. He was giving her himself without fear or misgivings.

It was openly mind-blowing feeling that he trusted her, without fear that she would throw it back in his face. He didn't ask for her to show it back or tell him how she felt in return; he was just showing her how he felt.

He gave her the power in the relationship to make her own decisions. His jealousy might have driven him to tinker with her car and butt into her meeting with Liam, but for a Porter, used to having his own way and knocking any obstacle out of his path instead of going around it, he had showed remarkable restraint.

"I love you." She let go of the hatred she had felt for herself for not protecting Valentine better, for not being strong enough to get away from Scott, for being the weak, useless victim he had made her believe she was.

Her struggle and suicide attempts hadn't been because of Scott, but because she wasn't able to forgive herself. All the group members at her support meetings, friends at work, and her therapist had told her it wasn't her fault; she hadn't believed them until now, as Tate showed her what real love was.

Evil intentions masquerading as caring cannot be recognized when good has never seen evil before. Scott had been her first brush with evil, and God willing, she would never see it again. If she did, she prayed she would be able to fight it better than she had the first time.

"I love you," Tate repeated her words without hesitation.

She undid his belt then unsnapped his jeans. "Make love to me."

Tate helped her shimmy out of her underwear before pressing her down onto the bench seat of his truck.

"I want you to know that I never fucked Cheryl without a condom, ever. Her having the clap was a rumor Jared started when she divorced him."

"I didn't ask, because I knew you wouldn't do anything to hurt me." Her lack of trust in Tate had been what had destroyed her life, and she would never make that mistake again.

"You're so beautiful. It hurts my dick to look at you. Even after I fuck you, I can't breathe because I want you again."

"Me, too...I thought I could never enjoy sex, and now I can't get enough of you. No one ever made me feel the way you do or ever will." She smoothed his plaid shirt off his shoulders that gleamed in the moonlight.

He made her feel soft and feminine.

Sutton shuddered as he unzipped her dress, sliding it off in the tight confines of the truck. She wanted to make love to him until the only woman he could remember being in his arms was her.

She had learned his sweet spots. His neck was sensitive, which she now delicately licked the side of, gently biting down and marking him as hers. Any woman in town who tried to take Tate from her would find she wouldn't stand around and let them take him from her again. She would fight tooth and claw to keep what was hers, and Tate was hers.

Tate rose up over her, sliding his dick into her, his hand going to the door over her head to brace himself to not smother her with his weight.

"Careful. I don't want to fall," Sutton warned as he began to thrust into her.

He buried his face in her neck. "If we fall, we'll do it together. Nothing can hurt us again." He took her hand, lifting it to his mouth, tracing the scarred flesh of her wrist with his lips. "Together, Sutton."

"Together." She wiggled under him, driving him deeper inside of her until she didn't know where he ended and she began, melding them together as one.

He groaned as he climaxed, and watching his face and the expression of pure pleasure drove her to find her own orgasm. They then lay on the bench seat, enjoying holding each other.

Both of them jumped when a sharp rap on the window startled them. Tate reached down, handing her the dress that had fallen to the floorboard. He rose up enough for her to cover herself before straightening to roll down the window.

Sutton wanted to die of embarrassment when she saw the sheriff staring into the dark cab.

"A little too old to be making out at Lookout Point, aren't you, Tate?" Knox didn't make an attempt to hide his amusement.

Tate unconcernedly zipped himself back into his jeans. "I've seen some of those parties you and The Last Riders throw at the lake. At least I made sure no one was around."

The huge sheriff's eyes narrowed in anger. "Really? Then how did I sneak up on you without you noticing?"

"I noticed. I just wasn't finished."

Sutton's mouth dropped open. She reached out, smacking him on the back of his head.

Knox started chuckling when Tate tried to catch her flailing hands.

"I'll leave you to deal with her. Keep an eye out and remember we haven't caught that shooter. Wouldn't want you to get shot in the back while you're...finishing." With that, the sheriff returned to his squad car.

"I can't believe you." Sutton quickly pulled on her dress before reaching down to snag her panties. Raising her hips, she put them on as she listened to Tate laugh his head off at her.

"You jerk, quit laughing. Daffy Duck has more sense than you!"

"Come on, Sutton; it was funny as shit. You should have seen your face when he was standing there. It was your idea to make out in my truck, so don't blame me for giving in," he snickered.

Sutton was about to let him have it again when a strange expression crossed his face.

"What's wrong?"

"Nothing." He started the truck, turning it around and driving down the mountain with hair-raising speed.

"Tate, you're scaring me."

"You mind if we spend the night at my house?"

"No, why?"

"I heard the death bells earlier today, then again when we were in the bar. I want you safe at the house where I can protect you and the others better. Dustin's at the house with Logan and Holly, but we know Greer's in town."

Sutton didn't question the request. He had once told her he heard death bells when someone he knew died. It wasn't folklore among mountain people, but a strong belief handed down through generations.

"I don't mind," she assured him as they drove toward his house.

He had her call and warn Greer, who answered the phone, obviously drunk, but when she conveyed Tate's message to be careful, he sobered instantly.

"He want me to come home?"

"No, stay put. I don't want you giving anyone an easy target! I'm headed home. I'll stay until you get back tomorrow," Tate answered. Sutton had put him on speaker phone so Tate could talk to him as he drove.

"Be careful, brother. I don't know what I would do without you." Greer's affection for his brother almost made him seem normal. And then…he blew the kind thought. "I'd have to do all the work without you."

"See you in the morning." Tate nodded at her to disconnect the call.

"Your brother is an asshole."

"He's not so bad."

"Yes, he is. He's the most self-absorbed man I've ever met."

Tate didn't try to argue back. Even he had to admit she was right.

When they pulled up in front of Tate's house, the yard flooded with lights from all direction.

"I bet your electricity bill would feed the homeless for a month."

Tate grinned as he opened the truck door for her. Sutton slid across the bench seat into his waiting arms, and he gently lifted her to the ground.

"Wait until I go to the hardware store and buy some for your yard. I like to know if someone comes snooping around."

"It has to go off if an animal triggers it."

"They do all the time. It makes them a better target," he said unrepentantly.

"We need to have a serious talk about your views on wildlife."

"I don't care if they have two or four legs. I'm going to blow anything away that comes near the house."

Sutton shook her head. She was never going to change his attitude. She was either going to have to deal with it or circumvent. She decided to buy trash cans with lids that locked. If she didn't, her poor possum was going to be stew meat with the way Tate threatened.

She nodded toward the house. "Dustin's watching from the window."

"I know." Tate kissed her soundly before releasing her.

She walked toward the front porch on her unsteady heels, nearly falling, but Tate caught her, lifting her high into his arms and carrying her the rest of the way.

"I could get used to this," she teased.

"I'll always be there to carry you whenever you need me. Even when you don't, I'll be there."

Dustin was still watching them with his shotgun in his hands, ready to protect them if needed.

"The Porters aren't perfect. You're mean, stubborn, and would rather shoot someone when you're mad, but you're the perfect man for me." Even as she said it, she couldn't understand her reasoning.

He arrogantly summed it up with six words. "I'm the only man for you."

Even a priceless vase had a crack or two.

"Tate, believe me, no one is like you."

⊗ ⊗

Tate sat up straight in bed, stumbling from the bed he went to the living room so he wouldn't wake Sutton. Jerking the curtain back he stared out the window, his shotgun in a tight grip, he had heard the bells for the third time. Death had found his victim.

CHAPTER TWENTY-TWO

Sutton stood in the kitchen, watching Dustin, Tate, and Logan eat breakfast while she drank her coffee.

"Are you sure you don't need me to help with the dishes?" she asked Holly.

"No, I'm almost finished. This will be much easier after next week. Tate's having a new kitchen installed."

She was struck by how pretty Holly was when she smiled. Sutton couldn't find it in herself to be envious of the woman, though. She was just too nice.

Holly was constantly trying to please the men as if she was unsure of her position in the tight-knit family. She wore a pair of jeans that showed her curvy butt, but she had put on an oversized top as if she was trying to hide the size of her overlarge breasts. Sutton had to admit she envied that problem.

The sound of a pickup outside had Logan jumping up from the table to look out the window.

"It's Uncle Greer, and he has that stupid Diane with him." Logan ran back to the table to finish his cereal.

"And so it begins…" Sutton murmured.

"What did you say?"

Sutton nodded toward Logan. "The next generation of Porters."

Holly laughed. "I've thought the same thing myself many times. As long as he turns out more like Dustin and Tate, he'll be fine."

"He doesn't take anything from Greer?"

"Just one thing, and I'm trying to nip it in the bud."

Greer opened the door, completely taking over the room with his appearance. Diane came in after him, dressed in a pair of shorts that showed the cheeks of her ass and a T-shirt that was completely inappropriate for the cool weather outside.

"You all still eating? We had breakfast at the diner." Glancing down at the table, Greer surveyed his brothers eating oatmeal doused in fruit. "Mine was better cold than that crap you're eating."

Sutton's hand tightened on her coffee cup at seeing the hurt look on Holly's face.

"Eating at the diner is what's putting that spare tire around your waist." Tate's harsh voice left no one in the room in doubt that he wasn't going to tolerate anyone mistreating Holly.

Diane's arms circled Greer's waist from behind, her hands splaying open on his flat stomach. "He hasn't got an ounce of spare flesh. I can vouch for that," she purred.

Sutton turned to place her empty cup on the counter, swallowing hard when she saw the flash of emotion on Holly's face that brought dread to her heart. The sweet woman was in love with the worst Porter brother.

Tate's cell phone broke the uncomfortable silence. Everyone in the room listened as he talked.

"Hey, Rachel…" His voice broke off as he listened to whatever Rachel was saying. "No one saw anything?"

Sutton's stomach sank.

"Call me if you hear anything else." Tate disconnected the call, staring at them grimly. "Holly, take Logan into the bedroom and turn on a movie for him."

"Let's go, Logan." Holly ushered the boy out of the room.

As soon as they heard the bedroom door close, Tate told them the awful news. "Mick found Kyle Hayes dead this morning, sitting in his truck in back of Rosie's bar."

Kyle Hayes was the younger cousin of Asher and Holt. He was just a young boy when Sutton had left town. He was one of the only Hayeses who had been allowed to attend school in town. She had often seen Kyle trailing after his much older cousins with hero worship in his eyes.

"They'll be out for blood."

"Yes, they will." Tate's face became even grimmer, frightening Sutton. "I saw him parking his truck as we were leaving. The parking lot was full, so he parked in the back. Rachel said Knox told her he was stabbed to death."

"Kyle knew how to take care of himself. He had to have known the killer, or he would never have gotten close enough to him to do any damage." Greer's face had gone white. "After the fight we had with Asher and Holt in the bar, you know who they're going to blame."

"Us," Tate confirmed everyone's worst fear.

"Knox can tell them he saw us at Lookout Mountain, and Diane can vouch for Greer being with her," Sutton spoke up.

"They aren't going to believe we didn't have anything to do with Kyle's murder."

Sutton had the awful feeling Tate was right.

When he stood up and put on his hat, she placed a hand on his arm. "Where are you going?"

"I'm going to go talk to Asher. If I don't make him believe me, there's going to be a blood bath."

"No!" Sutton gripped his arm more tightly. "Let Knox go."

"He's not going to believe Knox." Tate pried her hand off his arm. "I have to go, Sutton."

"I'll go," Greer volunteered.

"No, I want you here. You take care of the family." Hidden in his words was 'if I don't come back'.

"Tate…please, don't go."

"Walk outside with me." He took her hand, pulling her behind him as he went outside. "It's going to be all right."

Sutton pointed at his black eye. "They're not going to believe you. They're going to still be mad about the fight last night, and with their cousin being dead a few hours later…They just aren't going to believe you."

"I'll make them believe me. They both know one thing about the Porters: we're not cowards. I stand a better chance convincing them we had nothing to do with Kyle's death if I stare them in the eye and tell them the truth."

"Will you at least call Knox and tell him where you're going?"

"That, I can do."

"I'm going to be worried sick until you get back."

"Then keep yourself occupied. Clean the…"

Sutton's eyes narrowed. "Choose your next words carefully."

Tate, unlike Greer, wasn't a stupid man. "Find something you want to do to keep yourself occupied."

"I'll call Cheryl and have lunch with her. She's been calling, and I've been putting her off. I can pick up some flood lights while I'm in town."

"What made you change your mind about the flood lights?"

"The killer. He's taking everyone out in the dark."

Tate frowned. "You're right; all the attacks are happening during a certain time of night."

Sutton nodded. "He doesn't want to be seen."

"Either that or he's busy during the day." Tate placed his hand on the nape of her neck, pulling her close. "Borrow Holly's car to drive into town. I'll fix yours tonight."

"So, you're admitting to disabling my car?"

Tate gave her a quick kiss. "I'm a Porter; I never admit to a thing."

ೞ ಅ

Sutton waited patiently for Cheryl at King's restaurant. There was a large group of women sitting at one of the tables in the bar. Their loud laughter was being ignored by the owner of the restaurant. She understood why when he went to the table and talked to one of the beautiful women. It was obvious by the closeness between them that they were a couple.

Cheryl came rushing in, sitting down across from her. "Sorry I'm late. The store's busy."

Another round of laughter had Cheryl looking over at the group of women. Sutton wondered if they were eating as much as they were using the opportunity to gossip.

Cheryl's shoulders dropped as she gave the waitress her order.

"Something wrong?" Sutton asked after the waitress left.

"Those are the wives of The Last Riders'. The redhead is Evie. She's the owner's wife."

"So? Don't you get along with them?"

"No."

"I recognize Lily and Beth Cornett and Winter Simmons. From what I remember about them, I can't imagine them being hateful toward you."

Cheryl shrugged, avoiding her gaze. "I was kind of mean to a couple of them when I went through my divorce."

"I'm sure they understand it was a difficult time for you."

"I was with Cash."

Sutton was crushed for Rachel. "He slept with you after he and Rachel were married?"

"No…no. Before." Cheryl looked miserable at the admission.

"You were with Tate, too."

"Yes."

"I'm sitting here with you, and I still consider you my friend."

"You always were a sucker," Cheryl said, tears brimming in her eyes.

"No, I discovered good friends are hard to come by."

Cheryl smiled at her in relief.

They ate their lunch, and it was when they finished and were leaving that Sutton noticed Cheryl wince as she opened the door to the restaurant for them to exit.

"What's wrong?"

"Nothing. I lifted a heavy box at work and must have strained something."

Sutton stopped dead in her tracks, critically looking Cheryl over.

"Don't lie to me." Sutton reached out to touch a barely noticeable bruise on her jawline.

Cheryl took a step back from her touch. "I fell the other night when I drank too much…"

Sutton remembered the excuses all too well. She broached the subject carefully, the way she wished someone had taken the time to do with her.

"Cheryl…I know what it looks like when someone is hurting you."

Immediately, Cheryl went on the defensive. "Don't be crazy, Sutton. I'd call the sheriff if someone touched me…"

"I know," Sutton stressed.

Cheryl didn't understand what Sutton was trying to tell her until Sutton grabbed her hand, preventing her from continuing to walk.

"I know, Cheryl. I. *Know.*"

Cheryl stopped, comprehension finally dawning, and she held Sutton's hand tighter.

"You were abused by your husband?"

"For over ten years," Sutton admitted without embarrassment. It was Tate who had finally suceeded in convincing her she had been a victim. It was her chance now to pass along the same gift to Cheryl.

"It was my fault. I shouldn't have been flirting while I was working."

It sickened Sutton at the excuses men made to hurt women, convincing them they were the cause of their own pain.

"Listen to me, Cheryl. *Nothing* you did would give him the right to lay a hand on you."

"I need the job." Another excuse. Sutton remembered the many she had made for Scott, but she had never given herself one reason for why she should put up with the torture she had tolerated.

"We're going to go talk to Knox."

"I have to finish work. Today's payday. I need the money, Sutton. I'll go talk to Knox when I get off. At least I'll have enough money to live off for a couple of weeks."

"I'll lend you money until you find another job. I'll help—"

Cheryl stubbornly shook her head. "I'm getting my money. I worked for it."

Sutton bit her lip. She didn't want to push Cheryl too hard, or she could refuse to go to Knox for help.

"Okay. How much longer before you get off?"

"Four hours."

"Then I'm not leaving your side. I need to pick up some things for my house and Tate's. Will Jared get suspicious if I hang out that long?"

"No, I always have customers who stay and talk."

"All right. I hope you have a lot of flood lights."

"Flood lights? What do you need flood lights for?"

"Tate wants to set them up at my house so he can catch a possum." She was indirectly telling her that she and Tate were living together.

"Oh." Cheryl didn't seem thrilled by the information. "So, you won't be leaving to go back to Calfironia? When I move in with your friends, you won't be there?"

Sutton had believed she was upset about Tate living with her; however, it was because she had decided to move and wouldn't know anyone.

"No, but my boss is driving up next week. I'll introduce you. I think it would be a good idea for you to go ahead and leave."

"If I can manage to get my paycheck away from Jared, I might drive back with him," Cheryl conceded.

Sutton wound her arm through hers. "I'm not going to leave you alone until after you see Knox."

"Be careful. Jared's got a temper."

Sutton reached out and touched the faint bruise that Cheryl had tried to hide with her makeup.

"Jared's the one who needs to be careful. The next time he thinks he's going to touch you, he's going to find out something I wished I had known."

"What's that?"

"You're not alone."

CHAPTER
TWENTY-THREE

"Is that all for you?" Jared asked when she laid another item on the counter.

"No, not yet. Where's the rope?"

"Last aisle on the left."

Sutton took her time looking at the rope, as if it was the most important decision she was ever going to make. She picked up a bright yellow one that looked as if Tate could somehow use it. She frankly had no idea, nor did she about the numerous other items she had pretended to be shopping for. She would have come out cheaper if Cheryl had taken her offer of money.

Sighing, she turned to go back to the register, bumping into Jared who came up behind her.

"That it? We're about to close."

"Okay. I think that's the last of it." She followed him to the register, paying him after he rang up her purchases.

While Cheryl bagged her purchases, she saw Jared begin to take the receipts out of the cash register.

"Go ahead and lock the door after her," Jared ordered.

"Cheryl, is there a bathroom I could use?"

"Sure. It's at the back of the store on the left. It's next to Jared's office."

"I'll show you. I'm going to my office to count the money. When you're done locking up, Cheryl, come back and pick up your paycheck."

"Okay."

Ignoring the aggravated frown Jared threw her, she followed him to the restroom. She made sure he went into his office before she entered the bathroom, locking the door behind her. Taking out her cell phone, she saw several missed calls, calling Tate she knew he was going to be angry she hadn't already done so. She was angry at herself, She knew better than to try to take on a monster by herself.

He picked it up on the first ring.

"Tate..."

"Where are you? I got home and found out you weren't there. Then I went to your house, and you're not here, either."

She lowered her voice. "I know I'm not at home," she snapped. "Listen to me. I'll explain later. I'm still at the hardware store with Cheryl. Could you come and meet me outside? I found out Jared's been hurting Cheryl, and I've talked her into going to Knox when she gets off. I'd feel better if you were here."

"Get the fuck out of there. I'll be right there. I'm going to call Knox."

Tate hung up before she could say anything. She flushed the toilet and washed her hands before opening the door, coming face to face with a furious Jared.

His hand struck out, hitting her in the face and knocking her into the sink. She barely managed to catch herself before she hit her head.

"Jared, have you lost your mind?" Cheryl shoved him out of the way, rushing to help Sutton to her feet.

"You dumb cunt, do you think I'm stupid?" Jared yelled at Cheryl.

"Can I answer that question for you?" Sutton regained her balance from her reeling senses. Her fingers went to the blood running from her split lip.

Jared pulled out a gun his protruding belly had hidden.

"I wish you had told me he had a gun."

"Everyone in Kentucky has a gun. I didn't know he was carrying it around on him." Cheryl edged closer to her for protection. The simple movement empowered Sutton. Her friend thought she was strong enough to get them out of this terrifying position.

"Tate's on his way."

"Good. I have a score to settle with him, too. He's the last one on my list. I would have taken care of him the night I killed Lyle, but I wanted Knox to lock his ass up for a while."

"*You* killed Lyle? Why?"

"Because, when I killed you, I wanted everyone to believe a crazy shooter was picking his victims at random."

"You're right about the crazy!" Cheryl yelled. "Did you kill Helen Stevens and Kyle, and shoot at Rider, too?"

"Yeah. What do you not understand? Mrs. Stevens gave you the advice to divorce me, remember? I heard them talking to you at the diner one day. That old bitch won't be giving anyone advice anymore. Rider fucked you. I heard someone coming, or I would have gotten him. You saved me the trouble of going after Tate. Now I can kill all three of you and find you in the morning when I open the store, a love triangle gone wrong."

"No one will believe that!"

"Why not? Everyone in town knows what the Porters are capable of. I'm surprised he's still breathing after Kyle showed up dead. I'm disappointed in Asher and Holt; I was hoping they would take him out for me." Jared's evil gaze showed he had lost all reason. "Move." He waved them out of the bathroom, pointing the gun at them.

Sutton and Cheryl gingerly stepped around Jared as he backed up, motioning them to his office. They went inside, and he shut the door behind them. He then went to a row of security screens, flicking them on.

"That's disgusting." Sutton couldn't hold back her contempt when she saw one was of the bathroom.

"You want disgusting? Look at this." Jared opened a drawer, rifling through several tapes before picking one out and putting it in a VCR. The video came up of Cheryl and Tate having sex in a bedroom.

"You put a camera in my bedroom!" Cheryl screeched.

"Shut up! You're lucky I didn't put this up on the internet. The only reason I didn't was because what man would get off watching you?"

"If you watched that tape, then you saw Tate didn't have a problem, which is more than I can say about you!"

Sutton knew Cheryl was furious and angry, but she needed her not to incite Jared any further. Sutton prayed Knox would be here soon, but with them locked in an office with no windows, she knew the chances of her and Cheryl getting out alive were small.

She sat down in the chair by Jared's desk and started laughing helplessly.

Jared trained the gun on her. "What in the fuck are you laughing at?"

"I tried to commit suicide six years ago, and I haven't really cared if I was alive or dead. Now, when I finally do, you're going to kill me. Don't you find that hilarious?"

"I don't." Cheryl started crying. "Why did you try to kill yourself?"

"Because my husband tried to kill me. He killed my daughter. He shot himself because he was too much of a coward to face what he had done. He was just like Jared."

"I'm no coward. I'm not going to kill myself. I won't have to as soon as Tate gets here. I'll kill all three of you then take off. Diane is cooking dinner for me; she'll be my alibi."

The three of them watched as Tate came to the front door, trying to open it. When he couldn't, all three of them watched as he walked around the building to the backdoor, alone and unarmed.

Jared shot the security screens and ripped the cords out of the wall. "Can't have Knox looking through the security footage."

"How are you going to explain those tapes?"

"Evidence for my divorce. I just didn't throw them away, because I didn't want to embarrass Cheryl."

The man seriously believed he was going to be able to lie his way out of a triple murder. Maybe he could since he had gotten away with killing several people in town.

Jared ushered them into the other room where Tate was banging on the back door.

"Open it." He motioned to Cheryl. "Let him in and don't open your mouth, or I'll shoot you where you're standing."

Sutton started to scream a warning but Jared grabbed her, placing his hand over her mouth.

Cheryl swung open the door, barely managing to move out of the way as Tate ran inside.

"Shut the door and lock it!" Jared screamed at Cheryl. "Stop, Tate, or I'll blow your fucking brains out."

Tate stopped. "Let her go, Jared. Your problems with Cheryl don't involve me and Sutton."

"They involve you. I saw you fucking my wife. Maybe I should tie you and Cheryl up, and you can watch me fuck Sutton. How do you think you would like that, Tate? I bet she would, wouldn't you?" He bent down, swiping his tongue against the length of her neck.

"You're going to die for that," Tate promised.

"The ones who are going to die tonight are you and these two whores." Jared pointed the gun at Tate and squeezed the trigger.

Sutton grabbed his arm, pushing his hand with the gun toward the ceiling.

"Stupid bitch." Jared flung her away from him. Tate caught her in his arms, holding her close for a brief second, then pushed her behind his back.

"You're going to have to kill me to get to her," Tate vowed.

"I have no problem with that." Again, Jared pointed the gun at Tate, but before he could pull the trigger again, a voice from behind him spoke up.

"I have a problem with you trying to kill my brother. Lay that weapon down, or I'll blow your motherfucking head off." Greer moved to stand closer to Jared, placing his rifle against Jared's skull.

Dustin fanned out to the left, pointing his shotgun at Jared's stomach. Jared jumped when Dustin and Greer both pumped their shotguns.

"When we get done with these shotguns, you'll be declared brain dead, and they will be parceling your organs to everyone in Kentucky who needs them."

"I'd listen, Jared. Put your gun down before I take my shot. I'm getting bored listening to them bragging about how they're going to take you out." Knox sidled around them, his weapon pointed at Jared's face.

Jared's eyes ping-ponged between the men circling him, then he tossed his gun down onto the floor.

The room filled with gunfire.

"What the fuck!" Tate shoved Sutton into a stack of boxes. One had shards of cardboard sheared off as a bullet struck it.

"Who in the hell's shooting?" Greer roared as he and Dustin found cover.

Knox grabbed Jared, shoving him toward the door that led outside, but a spray of bullets stopped him.

"Stay where you are, Knox. Jared isn't going anywhere."

Tate pushed Sutton down farther, leaning over her to cover her with his body.

"Asher, is that you?" Tate yelled out.

"Stay out of this, Tate. Call your brothers off. Jared is mine. He killed Kyle. After you left, someone called to tell me they saw Kyle and Jared talking in the parking lot last night."

"That doesn't mean he killed him," Tate argued back.

"He did. He bragged about it to me and Cheryl," Sutton whispered.

Tate changed tactics. "Let me get my woman and brothers out of here, and you can have Jared. You'll save me the trouble."

"What about you, Knox?"

"I would have given him to you if you had asked. But that was before you shot at me!" he roared.

"I'm going to suck a shotgun if you all don't shut up." Greer stood and, taking aim, shot Jared, who fell to the ground.

"He shot him." Sutton couldn't believe Greer had unconcernedly taken Jared's life in the blink of an eye.

"I'm surprised it took him so long."

"You son of a bitch! He was ours!" Holt came out from behind a barrel.

"I was tired of waiting for everyone to talk him to death."

"Greer, you're under arrest," Knox snarled.

"Why? I saved Treepoint thousands of dollars in court costs. If you hurry, they may be able to save his organs."

Sirens came from outside and bullhorns sounded.

"Your deputies are always late," Greer taunted.

"That's the state police, you idiot. My deputies are holding the crowd back. I didn't figure I needed them when I have half the fucking town in here with loaded guns."

He touched the radio on his shoulder. "Mike, send in the EMTs. Tell everyone to stand down. The threat is over."

"Sure thing, Sheriff."

Knox took his hand off the radio. "We have about sixty seconds to get our stories straight. Which one of you wants to take credit for killing him?"

Greer's chest puffed out. "I did it. I'll take credit for it."

Holt stepped forward. "I will. That way, I can claim I was temporarily insane when I found out he killed Kyle. No one on the jury will send me to jail."

Knox turned to look at Greer. "You good with that?"

"Fuck no. I did it. I want credit for it."

"You think the jury will let you off? The Hayeses are related to half of the town, and they all hate the Porters. They'd cheer when they sent you off to prison."

"Dammit." Greer tossed his shotgun to Holt. "I'll be wanting that back."

Holt tossed him his. "I'll be wanting mine back."

Knox turned to look at Cheryl questioningly.

"I didn't see a thing. I was hiding in the bathroom where I couldn't see."

"Sutton?"

"I couldn't see, either," Sutton said. She couldn't feel sorry for the man bleeding out on the floor. He had killed to hide his tracks for no other reason than his pride had been injured when Cheryl had divorced him.

"Everyone else try to say as little as possible. Greer, that means you, too."

"Dustin, if Greer opens his mouth to say more than yes or no, shoot him."

"Tate! Dustin isn't going to shoot his brother." Sutton could tell from Greer's rebellious expression he wasn't going to keep quiet, and from Tate's grim expression, he knew it, too.

Knox looked out the door. "They're here," he warned.

Before anyone could guess his intentions, Tate grabbed Dustin's rifle and moved to stand behind Greer. Using the butt of the rifle, he knocked Greer in the back of his head, and Greer fell to the ground, out cold.

Sutton stared in shock at the merciless way Tate had dealt with Greer. Even Knox and the Hayeses stared at him speechlessly. The only one not surprised was Dustin.

Tate shrugged, unconcerned his brother was unconscious on the floor. "Problem solved."

CHAPTER
TWENTY-FOUR

"How is he?" Tate shut Greer's bedroom door before answering Holly.

"Go to bed. He's fine. He's watching some television. It'll take more than a crack upside the head to keep Greer down for long. If he tries to get out of bed, I'll shoot him. That'll make him stay put for a few days."

"Does he need anything? I could make him something," she offered sweetly.

"I wouldn't go in there if I was you. He's not in a good mood. I took him some water and gave him a pain killer, so he'll be fine until morning."

"The pharmacy was closed, so how did...?" Holly broke out, sniffing the air. Her hands went to her hips. "I told you no smoking that stuff in the house."

"I only gave him one. I figured he deserved it for taking out Jared."

"That's the last thing he needs with a head injury."

"Tell that to Greer. Logan's spending the night with his grandmother, because we didn't want to wake him when we finished at the hospital. It was easier to give in to Greer than him getting upset when I kept telling him no."

"You should have told me. I don't have a problem telling him no."

Tate laughed. "If he wants another, I'll let you have the fun of telling him," he promised.

He started to go into his bedroom where Sutton was changing when Holly reached out, forestalling him.

"Tate, if I'm in the way...now that you and Sutton are together...I could move into town." The sincerity of her offer had him placing his hand over hers.

"Don't even think about it. You're not going anywhere. Sutton and I are going to make our home at Pap's house. It's close by and gives us time to be alone before we start our family. I don't think Sutton would want to live with three men in one house, especially if one of those men is Greer," he teased.

"You're sure?"

"I'm sure. When Greer is feeling better, he and Dustin can help move me out. I want you to take my bedroom."

"I can't do that!" she protested.

"Yes, you can. I'm not giving you a choice. That room you're sleeping in isn't big enough for you. Go to bed and get some sleep. All your chicks are home for the night," he said gently.

Holly was the most caring woman he knew. She was always willing to sacrifice what she wanted if she thought someone else needed it more. She had no blood relatives of her own and was alone, so she clung to them and cared about them. Tate was going to make damn sure she was taken care of. They might not be blood, but she was family.

"Goodnight."

"Night, Holly."

Tate went in his bedroom where Sutton was sitting on the side of the bed with a towel wrapped around her, brushing out her hair.

She looked up when he closed the door. "How's Greer?"

"Mean as ever."

Sutton's lips twitched.

Tate walked forward, stopping in front of her. "How are you?"

"Fine. A little shaken up. I don't know which was worse: finding out Jared killed all those people or that he was only killing them so he could kill Cheryl."

"He was the only man in town who was stupider than Greer."

Sutton laughed. Wincing, she touched her split lip. "How do you always manage to make me laugh?"

"I don't know. It's probably the hillbilly in me." He sat down next to her on the bed, taking the brush from her. He brushed her hair back from her neck, placing teasing kisses against the nape.

"I'm sorry I didn't call you sooner." She shivered against him. "I should have known better."

"Mmm-hmmm..." Tate continued kissing her.

"You're not going to yell at me?"

Tate lifted his head in surprise. "Why would I yell at you?"

"Well...I almost got killed."

"Sutton, I'm so happy that you're alive, sitting here beside me, that I can't find any anger in me. Maybe I can tomorrow, but I doubt it. Porters always run into trouble."

"I'm not a Porter," she whispered.

"Not yet."

"Tate, are you asking me to marry you?"

"No, I'm telling you that, when you're ready, we'll go down to the courthouse and get hitched." With the faintest touch, he kissed the corner or her mouth. "If Jared was still alive, I'd shoot him because I can't kiss you the way I want. Get in the bed. I need to take a quick shower. I'll be right back."

"Okay."

Tate stood and stretched, smiling down at the woman he loved before turning to take off his clothes. Tears brimmed in his eyes at how close he had come to losing her again.

"Sutton?" He might have been successful hiding the emotion on his face, but his gruff voice gave him away.

"Yes?"

"Promise me something?"

"What?"

"Don't leave me again…I don't think I could take it."

He heard the squeak of the mattress as she got up, and then her arms circled his waist from behind.

He felt her lips press against his back. "I'm not going anywhere. I swear, Tate…I'll never leave you again." She laid her cheek against his back. "If I had fought to stay with you when I was seventeen as hard as I fought to stay away…"

He reached behind him, pulling her around to face him then pressing his hands against her shoulders to push her backward until she was against the bedroom wall.

"I heard the death bell when I was at the Hayes's house, I knew it was meant for you, that was the only the second time in my life I knew who Death was coming for. I should have listened to Pa. He told us all to keep what's ours. I will never, ever make that mistake again." He unwrapped the towel from around her, letting it fall to their feet before taking a red nipple in his mouth as his hand slid down to her thigh, lifting it to his hip.

"I thought you were going to take a shower?"

"I will when I'm done." He lifted her other thigh up to circle his waist.

"The bed's right there."

"We'll get there eventually. We have all night."

"Yes, we do."

Tate was done talking. He spread her thighs farther apart to give himself enough room to sink his cock inside of her, his knuckles brushing her clit, giving his woman enough stimulation to ease his entry. He didn't have to worry; he easily slid inside of her until his balls rested against her.

He braced his forearms on the wall as he began to grind himself into her, her thighs gripping him as the heels of her feet pressed down on his ass. He pumped into her harder as she held on to his shoulder, her nails digging into his flesh. Then he shoved her harder against the wall, trying to go higher, determined to reach every part of her he could, and her gasp had him raising his head from her breast.

"You okay?"

"Harder."

"If I fuck you any harder, we're going to go through this wall."

She giggled. "I can just see Greer's face if we fell into his bedroom."

"He's going to be in a shitty mood tomorrow."

"I thought the doctor said he would be feeling better tomorrow?"

"It's not going to be his head hurting."

Tate laid his head against the wall next to hers, desperately trying to hold back his climax until she came.

"Woman, you're making me work for it tonight."

Her pussy clenched on his cock.

"I don't want it to end…It feels…so good," she moaned.

"Like you're standing on the edge of a mountain, about to jump?"

"Yesss." Sutton's teeth clenched.

Sweat soaked their bodies, and her beaded nipples poked his chest.

He moved his head closer to whisper into her ear. "Fly with me..."

Sutton turned to stare into his eyes, their souls taking the leap together, jumping into the infinity of pleasure that had them clinging together as their orgasm entwined them. They flew then caught each other in gentle arms, gradually lowering themselves back to earth.

A loud pounding on the wall behind them had Tate placing a hand over Sutton's mouth to stifle her laughter.

He lifted his hand when they heard Greer's bedroom door slam closed.

"I guess he decided to sleep on the couch."

"I can't blame him. You were kind of loud."

"Me? I was not!"

"Woman, you were yelling at the top of your lungs."

She began hitting his shoulders playfully.

Tate set her down on her feet, backing away until he felt the bed behind him. She gave him a hard push with a wicked smile on her face. He toppled onto the bed, and she instantly straddled him, sitting on his stomach. He relaxed, staring up into her beautiful face.

He reached his hand up to cup her face. "I wish I had a camera. I'd take a picture of you right now. You're so fucking beautiful."

"You don't need a picture. I'll always be here. I had plenty of pictures, but none of them replaced you."

"Thank God you came home."

"I was home the second I saw you."

He had waited eighteen years for Sutton's return—hard, agonizing years for both of them. He was going to make sure each year they spent together would replace the time of heartache they had spent apart. If they lived a thousand years, maybe, just maybe, it would be even.

CHAPTER TWENTY-FIVE

"Come another inch closer, you little motherfucker."

Sutton took off running across the gravel driveway. Leaping up, she jumped onto Tate's back. "Don't you dare kill Brutus!"

"Woman, you know better than to startle a man when he has a gun in his hand!"

Her arms circled his neck. "Please, don't kill him. He's just trying to find a place to sleep. It's cold, and he's probably hungry."

"Do you see how fat that bastard is?"

"He's not the one scattering trash everywhere. I've been setting out a plate of scraps for him so he doesn't need to scatter trash everywhere." From Tate's angry reaction, she should have kept the last part to herself.

"Dammit, why don't you just open the door for him and invite him for dinner?"

Sutton settled her chin on Tate's shoulder as they watched the fat possum waddle across the yard toward the trash can, arrogantly ignoring them. Her possum definitely wasn't the smartest one in the woods.

A pine cone fell down from a tree a few feet, dropping onto the tin roof of the shed. Their eyes went up to the tree to see a raccoon sitting on a limb, watching them balefully. Everyone in the mountains knew that in the hierarchy of aggravating animals, a raccoon always ranked higher than a possum.

"I told you it wasn't Brutus. Isn't he cute?"

"No." He turned with her on his back and headed toward the house.

"Where are you going?"

"I'm locking you in the house while I take care of those two little—"

"You better not hurt a hair on Brutus or—"

"I have a name for that raccoon…dead meat."

He was almost to the house when a car pulled into the driveway, and Sutton instantly recognized the man and woman who got out.

"Put me down." She didn't wait, wiggling off his back to run into the house. Her shoe was on the first step when Tate caught her hand, making her come to stop.

"Sutton, they want to see you."

She angrily jerked around to face him, feeling betrayed. "You knew?"

"I saw them in the grocery store last night. They want to make things right. Look at them, Sutton." He gestured toward her parents. "I lost my parents without being able to say good-bye; I don't want the same to happen to you."

"I said my good-byes to them years ago," Sutton cried out, brushing her tears away, her gaze caught by her mother's.

She was crying so hard her shoulders were shaking as she wrung her hands at her waist. Her father stared at her steadily, his face a mask of pain.

She quit fighting against Tate's hold when it struck her how old they looked. Her mother had aged with wrinkles and lines making deep grooves in her skin. She was dressed in a casual dress that she once would have claimed she was too young to wear. Her hair had gone from the lustrous brown to all grey.

Time hadn't been any kinder to her father. His hair was just as grey, and the strong body he'd had when she had left was frail. Neither of her parents was well.

"Their grief is killing them, Sutton. It's all there if you look. The police notified them when Scott kidnapped you. They found out they had a granddaughter the same day they found out she had died."

"I can't," Sutton sobbed out.

"If you can't, I'm not going to force you." Tate released her hand, stepping back. "It has to be your choice to forgive them—I found that out the hard way with Rachel. I can't blame them, because I would have done the same if my daughter was seeing a man like me.

"I tried to do what I thought was best for Rachel, and it backfired on me. Cash was nearly killed Sutton, and Rachel ran off. I didn't know where she was for months. Just think, you've seen Cash and Rach together, how happy they are. I have a niece on the way now, and that all could have never happened because I interfered. I don't think deep down Rachel will ever forgive me. I broke her trust. I only had to suffer a few months before Rachel came back home, and it was a year before I think she said she forgave me.

"Your parents have been suffering for years. Put them out of their misery, Sutton. If not for them, for yourself. I don't want you to have any more regrets in your life.

"Do you love me, Sutton?" he asked abruptly.

"You know I do," she said achingly.

"I haven't asked you to take his wedding ring off, and I never will, even if you have to wear mine at the same time, because you have the right to hate that son of a bitch for what he put you through. Don't punish your parents because Scott's not here for you to take it out on him."

Sutton listened to Tate's words. The truth was ugly, and she didn't want to admit she had been blaming her parents for the mistakes she had made. They weren't blameless, but neither had they been fully responsible for her bad decisions.

There was only one person who had given Scott the power to destroy her.

Her own pride had been the cause of her destruction. She could have ran back home with Valentine, her father would have been able to protect them. He had the power to have kept Scott away, but to do that she would have had to admit to herself and them that she was powerless. The fierce independence she had fought to regain and anger over Tate, had her believing she couldn't accept their help.

Her parents' intentions hadn't been evil. They had tried to break her and Tate up because they had good intentions. Both her parents and Scott had tried to control her for different purposes, and it was time she recognized the difference and finally accept them deep in her heart, because she wasn't going to be able to change the past. Valentine wasn't coming back.

"I don't know if I can do this." She stood, trembling as her mother cried harder, waiting.

Suddenly, she took off running toward her mother, who held out her arms to her. "Mama! Daddy!"

Sutton felt herself enfolded in their loving arms that had been waiting to hold her again. For the first time in years, she found the peace that had been elusive.

"We're so sorry…" Her mother eyes were filled with sorrow.

"I should never have…" her father began.

"I shouldn't have…"

All three of them tried to talk at the same time when no words were needed. Whoever said there was no going home hadn't ever lived in her shoes. It had been a long, hard journey back, but her mountain blood hadn't let her stay away.

Tate was right. Thank God she had listened to the call that had sent her home to find the peace and love that had been waiting for her return. With everything she had lost, it had taken her returning to find what she needed the most.

Tate and her parents would help her find the joy of living again. The beautiful daughter she had been able to hold onto for such a short time would be waiting until they were together again. Until then, she was going to enjoy the happiness she had been given. This time, she was going to grab on, and even if Hell on Earth opened to swallow her whole, she wouldn't let go. She would brave the fires of Hell to keep what was hers. Even putting up with Greer would be worth it.

She felt Tate place his arm around her, giving her the support he thought she needed.

He was worth it and more. He was worth it all.

Epilogue

Tate leaned back against the hood of his truck, watching Sutton stand at the edge of the highest peak on Black Mountain. It had taken over two hours up the steep road to drive to the lookout point she wanted. It unsettled him the way she stood so close to the edge.

He crossed his arms over his chest to keep himself from reaching out to snatch her back into the safety of his arms. She hadn't told him why she had insisted they drive here today.

It was the first day of pretty spring weather they'd had, and the trees were just beginning to bloom. When he had parked the truck, his breath had caught at the breathtaking beauty of the blooming trees and clear sky.

Sutton had silently slid out of the truck, going toward the edge of the mountain. He had sensed she had wanted to be alone, and despite his wanting to be near her, he had held back.

He saw her hands rise to her waist, sliding off the wedding band on her finger before closing it into a tight fist in the palm of her hand. He held his breath when she took a step backward then one forward, her hand rising as she threw the ring high into the air.

His eyes followed the ring into the sky before it fell, disappearing from sight. When it could no longer be seen, she turned back to face him. He straightened from the truck, holding out his arms to her, and she ran toward him, jumping into his arms, her legs circling his waist.

Tate spun her in circles, his hat falling to the ground as she cupped his face with her hands.

"I'm ready to go to the courthouse."

He felt as if his chest was going to explode with the love he felt for this woman.

"Is this your way of proposing?" he teased.

"No, it's my way of telling you we're going to get hitched," she repeated the words he had told her at the beginning of winter. "I'm ready to become a Porter."

"I guess I'll accept your proposal, then."

"You better," she warned, "if you know what's good for you. Greer said he would kick your ass for me if you turned me down."

"He did?"

She nodded happily. "They're all going to meet us at the courthouse in a couple of hours."

"Confident of yourself, weren't you?"

"Where you're concerned, yes. I knew you wouldn't turn me down. You're not a stupid man." Her laughter never failed to touch his heart.

"It might have taken me eighteen years to marry you, but I eventually got it right."

National Domestic Abuse Hotline (thehotline.org)

1-800-799-7233

Books By Jamie Begley:

The Last Riders Series:
Razer's Ride
Viper's Run
Knox's Stand
Shade's Fall
Cash's Fight
Shade
Lucky's Choice

Biker Bitches Series:
Sex Piston
Fat Louise

The VIP Room Series:
Teased
Tainted
King

Predators MC Series:
Riot
Stand Off

Porter Brothers Trilogy:
Keeping What's His

The Dark Souls Series:
Soul Of A Man
Soul Of A Woman

About the Author

"I was born in a small town in Kentucky. My family began poor, but worked their way to owning a restaurant. My mother was one of the best cooks I have ever known, and she instilled in all her children the value of hard work, and education.

Taking after my mother, I've always love to cook, and became pretty good if I do say so myself. I love to experiment and my unfortunate family has suffered through many. They now have learned to steer clear of those dishes. I absolutely love the holidays and my family puts up with my zany decorations.

For now, my days are spent writing, writing, and writing. I have two children who both graduated this year from college. My daughter does my book covers, and my son just tries not to blush when someone asks him about my books.

Currently I am writing four series of books- The Last Riders, The Dark Souls, The VIP Room, and Biker Bitches series.

All my books are written for one purpose- the enjoyment others fi nd in them, and the expectations of my fans that inspire me to give it my best. In the near future I hope to take a weekend break and visit Vegas that will hopefully be this summer. Right now I am typing away on my next story and looking forward to traveling this summer!"

Jamie loves receiving emails from her fans,
JamieBegley@ymail.com

Find Jamie here,
https://www.facebook.com/AuthorJamieBegley

Get the latest scoop at Jamie's official website,
JamieBegley.net

Printed in Poland
by Amazon Fulfillment
Poland Sp. z o.o., Wrocław